I0752640

ACT OF MURDER

A Detective Al Warner Suspense

By

George A Bernstein

Award winning, Amazon #1 Best Selling Novelist

GnD Publishing LLC

Copyright © 2026 by George A Bernstein

All rights reserved. No part of this publication may be reproduced, distributed, or transmitted in any form or by any means, including photocopying, recording, or other electronic or mechanical methods, without the prior written permission of the publisher, except in the case of brief quotations embodied in critical reviews and certain noncommercial uses permitted by copyright law. For permission requests, write to the publisher, addressed "Attention: Permissions Coordinator."

GnD Publishing LLC
Palm Beach Gardens, Florida 33418

Publisher's Note: This is a work of fiction. Names, characters, and incidents are a product of the author's imagination. Locales and public names are sometimes used for atmospheric purposes and may have been altered to meet the demands of the story. Any resemblance to actual people, living or dead, or to businesses, companies, events, institutions, or locales is completely coincidental.

Book Layout ©2026 - www.whenweshare.com
Cover Design by Paradox Book Covers

Ordering Information: Quantity sales. Special discounts are available on quantity purchases by corporations, associations, Bookstores, and others. For details, contact the publisher.

Act of Murder/George A Bernstein—1st Edition
ISBN: 979-8-9871607-3-2

OTHER DETECTIVE AL WARNER NOVELS BY GEORGE A BERNSTEIN

Death's Angel – **AMAZON #1 Best Seller**
Book #1
Available in eBook, print, and audio

Born to Die
Available in eBook, print, and audio

The Prom Dress Killer
Available in eBook, print, and audio

White Death
Available in eBook and print

Sniper
Available in eBook and print

Taken
Available in eBook and print

Cold Vengeance
Available in eBook and Print

OTHER 5-STAR NOVELS BY GEORGE A BERNSTEIN

Trapped

A parapsychological Suspense

Winner in "The Next Great American Novel" contest

An Amazon Top 100 Novel

Available in eBook, print, and audio

A 3rd Time to Die

A paranormal Romantic Suspense

Available in eBook, print, and audio

Hidden Treasures-Amazon #1 Best Seller

An Erotic Romantic Suspense

Available in eBook, print, and audio

True Love? – Amazon #1 Best Seller

An Erotic Romantic Suspense

Available in eBook & print

ACT OF MURDER

~ 1 ~

Detective Al Warner's gray Dodge Charger screeched to a stop under the entry canopy of the Embassy Suites Hotel just as the golden disc edged above the horizon, partially masked by tall buildings of the eastern skyline. It seemed like every murder investigation began at dawn. Stepping from his custom coupe, he flipped his keys to the advancing valet.

"Just park her up the curb a bit. Ain't sure how long I'll be." He glanced at the double-glass doors. "What room?"

"Six-twenty-four, Detective," He slid into the seat. "Couple of your guys already up there." A grimace twisted his lips. "Heard it's pretty gruesome."

"Murder usually is, buddy," and he hurried through the entry, headed for the elevators. He'd spied the black CSU van and Jack Harris's gray Camaro perched along the drive. Warner hated being last on the scene, but he'd been out for an early run with Buff, his golden retriever, when the call came in, and he needed a quick shower and change of duds before he left. Eva and the baby were still asleep when he'd slipped out the door.

Exiting the elevator on Six, he had no trouble spotting the room, with a gaggle of street cops hovering in the doorway. He was there despite being Chief of Detectives for nearly eight years. Warner abhorred administrative work, preferring to work the crimes with a small cadre of his top detectives. Jack Harris was number one.

Warner strode into the one-bedroom suite and spotted his vinyl-gloved detective, Jack Harris, patrolling the floor, searching for clues. A CSU tech was videoing the entire scene, ready to film anything Harris might discover. Another was dusting for prints.

Harris looked up as Warner approached. "Vic's in the bedroom, Boss. The Hawk's with her, and the M.E. is on the way." He shrugged and sighed. "Damned attractive cougar, too. A real shame." He returned to inspecting the small sofa in front of the TV. "So far, no joy here."

With a nod, Warner turned toward the bedroom. *So, not the young beauty I'd expected.* Entering the room, he spied Moe Gold, nicknamed the Hawk, more for his keen eyes that missed little than the prominent hooked, Semitic beak, centered on his face. His diminutive CSU chief was inspecting the bed around the sprawled, naked figure of a lovely, onyx-haired woman.

"C'mon in, Detective," the short, wiry man muttered, not looking up. "COD appears to be strangulation, but there's also a knife wound to her heart, so an autopsy will have to verify what happened first." He stood and faced Warner. "From the lack of heavy bleeding, I suspect the knife was administered postmortem."

"Huh? Sounds like he was makin' a statement." Warner's fingers absently found the scar under the thick hair of his right temple. "I'm presuming it was a 'he,' suspectin' they were screwin'. Right, Moe?"

"Yes, though I can't rule out a Lesbian encounter until the M.E. does the exam. If they did have sex, it appear a condom was used, so my money's on a guy." His hand waved across the scene. "Not much here to go on, so far, but we'll keep at it. We'll vacuum the corpse to see if we can pick up anything, like skin cells or saliva, but don't hold your breath. This perp was professional and very careful."

"Great." Warner grunted and pivoted toward the outer room. "Another careful killer, which probably eliminates a crime of passion. Based on that knife wound, my gut tells me this could be a guy just gettin' started." Jack Harris met him at the doorway.

"The place it pretty well wiped down, Boss. Not sure we're gonna find anything probative." Withdrawing his tablet, Harris scrolled across the screen. "The vic is one Maria Santiago, forty-one, from Coral Gables. Appears, from her ID, to be an English prof at U or Miami. I sent it up to Tech, and they'll dig deeper. See if there were any guys in the picture. She paid for the room with a VISA card about ten p.m., and the night clerk says she seemed alone. Thought she was a bit buzzed and he guessed she opted not to drive home." He flipped to another screen page. "I did a preliminary scan of the CCTV cams and saw what appeared to be a guy, maybe five-ten to six-feet, black hair, wearing a brimmed hat. Couldn't get a facial, but we're pulling the recordings and sending 'em to Tech for a deeper dive." Harris glanced up and shrugged. "Not too optimistic, 'cause the guy clearly knew how to avoid being ID'ed."

"So," Warner scratched his chin, "nothin' to work on yet, other than a pretty, dead vic, and a signature that screams *serial.*" He glared around the room. "Damn, I hate these crazy bastards. If I'm right, this is our seventh mass killer in eight years. Each on a secret mission only they understood, and damned careful about leavin' clues. Shit!" He grabbed Harris's shoulder. "Keep at it, Jack. I don't want this one to drag out." He turned toward the door. "I'm gonna sic Olvida on seein' if he can find any other cases that might tie in with a similar MO. Get me your prelims ASAP. I'm headin' for the office."

"On it, Boos. I'll keep ya posted."

~ 2 ~

“Harris!” Warner stood in his office doorway. “My office. Olvida, you too. I need an update.”

“Coming, Boss.” Both detectives rose from their desks, gathered their gear, and hurried to meet their chief, who they found perched on a corner of his desk.

“So, whatcha got so far?” Warner’s eyes swept between them.

“Not as much as we’d like, Boss.” Harris paged through his Android. “Santiago was single, forty-one, an English Lit prof at Miami. Lived with another prof, Sherry Burns, in a fancy condo close to campus. Short preliminary interview with Burns ’cause she was so shaken up. Looks like the vic had an off-and-on boyfriends, Dave Sabbitt. Currently, off. Ralph,” glancing at Olvida, “is interviewing him tomorrow.”

“Know if he’s got an alibi?” Warner’s eyes found Detective Olvida.

“Seems to, Boss, but I’m verifying it.” Olvida studied his notes. “The roomie reluctantly admitted that Ms. Santiago would occasionally visit local bars, seeking ‘friends with benefits,’ to help pay for her doctorate degree at U of M.” He scanned a notebook. “Burns said she’d cautioned her to be careful, but Santiago felt she could spot a weirdo.”

“Yeah? She only needed to make a mistake once, and this mighta been it.” Warner rose and moved behind his desk. “Got a confirmed COD from the M.E. yet, Jack?”

“What it looked like, Boss. Strangulation. No apparent defensive wounds, so it musta been quick.”

"And the knife wound?" The Chief of Detectives eased back in his chair.

"Definitely post-mortem. The doc says it was done with precision, carefully."

"Kinda pierced, ya mean? Not like an angry stab wound?"

"Yeah, like that."

"So, the bastard's leavin' some kinda message." Warner knuckled his eyes. "That's why my gut says this is more'n a one-off." He sighed. "Either the first in a comin' series, or he's done it before." Eyebrows arched, he looked at Olvida. "Ya got anything on *that*, Detective?"

"Not yet, Boss, but we're still digging. Tech's sweeping the local data base, and the Hawk's loaded the details in the National Crime Register. So far, no joy." Olvida closed his pad and studied his boss. "You really feel this is the sign of a new serial loony?"

"My gut does. I'm gonna run it past Eva tonight. See if she's got any insights." He pulled over a yellow, lined pad and scrawled a note.

"How's she doing, Al?" Harris pushed out of his chair. "Recovered okay from that scary assassin's attempt to hurt you? I know it wasn't her first time."

"Yeah, it's been six months, but she's surprisingly tough. Bein' a psychiatrist, she's had associates she could talk with. Got the same kinda care she so often gave out."

"And that cute little girl of yours?" Olvida grinned.

"Andrea? Growin' like a weed, and gonna definitely have her momma's red hair. She's inta anything she can get her little mitts on."

"Gonna be a detective, just like papa, huh?" Harris chuckled.

"Maybe. Rather have her take after her beautiful mom than me, though, guys." Warner shook his head. "Married to her all these years now, and I still don't know how I got so lucky."

"Nobody deserves that more'n you, Boss." Harris patted Warner's arm, then turned for the door. "Anyway, Ralph and I'll keep digging. We're heading up to the campus tomorrow to interview some more colleagues. Be sure there wasn't any hanky-panky going on with one of her students."

"I was about to follow up with the Hawk and Tech, too, Boss," Olvida added. "We'll keep you posted."

"Right." Warner followed them to the door. "I wanna tie this one up, quick. I'm tired of havin' some loony fillin' body bags, with us havin' nothin' to chase."

"We'll get him." Harris paused, just outside Warner's office. "We always do, sooner or later. They rue the day they pull their shit on Al Warner's turf."

"Never knew a cop who hated this kind of bastard more than you, Boss." Olvida said as he pivoted toward his desk. "If this guy *is* serial, he's met his match."

"Okay, Okay. Great pep-talk guys." A grin. "Now let's see if we can keep the body bags to a minimum before we snag this nut."

Chuckling, they went their separate ways, each sure this was no run-of-the-mill murder. If so, this would be their seventh mass murderer in eight years. Each detective was intent in proving again, South Florida was the wrong place to ply their wares.

~ 3 ~

Al Warner inclined forward, forearms bracketing his plate, empty now but for smears of maple syrup and a few blueberry stains.

"Glad I took time for breakfast, babe." He grinned at Eva, then nodded toward Andrea, scrunched in her high-chair, licking her fingers. "Our daughter seemed to enjoy the pancakes as much as I did."

"Yes. You're usually in such a rush." Reaching across the glass top, her hand covered his, eyebrows arched. "So, I suspect you're looking for an opinion on a current case?"

"Yeah. You're take on the Santiago murder. The knife to the heart, post-mortem, seemed like some kinda signature ... or maybe a message." Warner studied her emerald eyes. "Some kinda cult thing? Or ...?"

"You're thinking another serial killer signature, Al?"

"Maybe. I got the guys lookin' for any similar vics. What d'ya think?"

"Not really enough to make an informed guess, darling, but if I had to ... maybe punishing women for someone in his or her life whose heart wasn't, in his view, in the right place." Eva sat back and folded her arms across her breast. "But at this point, that's just a wild guess at one of many possible triggers."

"I know." He sighed. "Unfortunately, we'll probably need another vic or two ta establish a pattern." Warner pushed up from his seat. "Not something I'm lookin' forward to." He circled the glass-top table and pulled his auburn-haired wife into his arms. "Glad I'm lucky enough to have a beautiful shrink to talk with about it, though." His nuzzle of her neck moved to a warm, gentle kiss. "My two gals keep me sane."

Gathering up his sport coat, his Glock .40 holstered in his shoulder rig, he bussed her cheek. "Gonna see what, if anything, the guys have dug up. You got appointments today?"

"Mostly in the afternoon, but I'll be home in time for the dinner you promised at Joe's Stone Crab. We still on for that?"

"Unless something big breaks. I'll pick up you, Adele, and Kira about six, and I promise I won't tell anyone that we're celebrating your fortieth." He chuckled. "You still pass for thirty-five in a breeze, babe."

Eva gave him a fierce hug. "Nice you're including Adele's sister."

He nodded. "Well, my two of my three most important women, you and Adele, almost share the same birthday, and Kira *was* a big help in breaking that Nazi vengeance case." A quick kiss, and he turned to leave, receiving a departing pat on his butt.

Warner grinned, and for the umpteenth time, reveled in how unexpectedly lucky he'd been to find such an exceptional wife, despite all the odds. And he was a dad, too!

~ 4 ~

Three months later

Warner entered the squad room and spied Jack Harris at his desk, tapping away at his keyboard. He strode the cubicle, defined by blue metal, glass-topped dividers, and Harris looked up at his approach.

"Anything new on our professor, Harris?" He perched on the corner of the desk. "We're runnin' outta time."

"Santiago?" He shrugged. "Nada, Boss. Olvida and I dug into everyone's alibi's and couldn't find a hint of anything." His Android in hand, the detective paged through several screens. "You know the boyfriend, Sabbitt, had a rock-solid alibi. Couldn't find anyone in the faculty or in her classes that might have a motive, and we dug pretty deep there. I was just working on a recap," nodding at his computer screen, "and the suggestion we kick it into cold cases." A hand ran through sandy hair, now streaked with gray. "Been over three months. No progress, no new related vics, which suggests it wasn't serial—"

"At least not here, in Florida." Warner rose from Harris's gray, metal desk. "Nothing from the National Data Base?"

"Not definitively, Boss. Three or four similar-type women over the past four years, but no signature knife to the heart. Scattered around the East and Midwest. Not enough for the Fibbies to connect them." A few screen shots flipped, and he set down the Android. "I checked with Agent Pauletti at the BAU at the outset, and our vic didn't ping anything on their radar." Harris scratched his freckled nose. "Maybe our vic was a one-off after all, but whoever the perp was, he didn't leave us anything to chase down."

"Yeah, maybe. But that knife in the heart said otherwise. Ya know the sayin' of someone who has been abused, 'You stuck a knife in my heart.' This sounds like that."

"Agreed." Harris pushed to his feet, and picked up his jacket. "Doesn't mean it's not a one-time act of some sorta vengeance, but I'll take Olvida and make one more pass at anyone connected." He shrugged into his jacket and picked up his shield and Beretta from his drawer. "But if we can't turn up anything new ...?"

Warner sighed. "Then kick it to Cold Cases. Don't mean it's gonna be outta my mind, though."

"No surprise there, Boss." Harris chuckled. "Been with you too long to expect anything else."

They exited his space together, and Harris beckoned Detective Rafael "Ralph" Olvida to join him.

Warner headed for his office. He had two new murder investigations to assign, one, a domestic turned violent in Miami Springs for Dean Beck, and the other, a drive-by, for a newly anointed homicide detective, Cairo Salinas. While new in Warner's department, Salinas had years on the street in Little Havana, where the shooting occurred. Residents of the area would respond better to a Hispanic cop ... if they responded at all. Drive-by's were among the hardest to crack because locals, either through fear or loyalty, seldom talked to the police. Success in those arenas required a good CI, and Warner gave Salinas the names of two he had there.

Most "regular" murders were solved in a matter of days. The usual perps weren't very careful about not leaving evidence. It was the ones like the strange death of Professor Santiago that took the most work, and sometimes were never cracked. Convictions of serial killer especially, often went unsolved. They were among the most difficult perps to snag.

Warner moved on with the normal business of the day for Miami-Dade Homicide, but that lovely, onyx-haired woman, sprawled naked on the bed, knifed in the heart, would linger in his thoughts for a very long time.

~ 5 ~

Two Years Later

Deena Wright perched on a bar stool and swiveled to face the happy-hour crowd at her favorite Brickell Avenue restaurant bar. She munched on her third slider, then licked her fingers and took a sip of her vodka gimlet. Disco dance music filled the air.

Some unfamiliar faces for a change, but nobody tonight from her law firm. Just as well, because the successful end of her drug class-action suit had fired up her libido. Fingers brushing back a lock of her inky, shoulder-length hair, she scanned the dimly lit room. Find the right guy, and he might get lucky tonight.

And there was a great candidate: tall, blonde, and damned handsome, despite a slightly oversized nose. Their eyes locked, he smiled, then ambled over and took a stool next to her.

"Hi, beautiful." Settled beside her Pilates-lithe body, he leaned back, elbows atop the bar's mahogany surface.

"Thanks." She chuckled. "But you can do better than that, a handsome guy like you."

"What?" Bushy blond eyebrows arched. "You don't think you're beautiful?"

"Don't hear that much at my age." She patted his arm, secure in that lie.

"Aw, c'mon. You're what a young buck would call a hot cougar." He smiled. "That's nothing but a compliment. A fine wine, well-aged." A glance from the corner of his eye. "I bet you're not even forty."

"That's sweet. So, how did we stumble into this inappropriate age subject? Not something women like to talk about, you know."

"Yeah. Sorry. Just trying to find a way to break the ice." He rotated toward her. "You remind me of someone very important in my life. I'm Jason, by-the-way."

"Deena."

He kissed her fingers.

"Friends call me Dee. So, is that a good or bad thing?"

"What?"

"Me, reminding you of someone?" Her lips tilted up as she finished her drink.

"What do you think, lovely Dee? How about I buy you another, find a table, and see?"

"Sounds like a good start." Her hand in his, they slipped off the stools, and he turned to the barkeep. "Another of whatever the lady is having, and a vodka and tonic for me, no lime."

A few minutes later, they set their drinks on a small corner table and he led her onto a crowded dancefloor where they swayed to the strains of a slow ballad. Dee snuggled close in his arms, her head nestled in the crook of his neck, the warmth of her body and the press of her breasts stirring his loins.

She's perfect.

After dancing to two slow ballads, whoever managed the sound tracks morphed into some rap-sounding thing, unsuitable for what the guy had in mind, so they returned to their table and sampled their drinks.

"So, what brings you to South Florida, Jason?" Her cobalt eyes searched his. "I sense this isn't home for you."

"Good guess, Dee. I'm here for ten days on a business

assignment." Their drinks finished, he signaled the bar for refills. "And you?" He curled her hand in his. "Florida is home for you, huh?"

"Yep. Born and raised in Miami." Their drinks arrived and she took a sip. "I'm an attorney at one of the bigger Miami firms, right here on Brickell." The rest of her gimlet finished, she grinned. "Let's have another. I'm celebrating."

"Happy to do that with you." He waved again at the bar and got a nod. "What's the occasion?"

"Just won a big class-action suit and made our clients—and the firm—a bucket of money." She took a big swig of her newly arrived vodka, then nibbled on peanuts from a small bowl. "Puts me on a fast track to named partner."

"Wow!" Jason raised his drink and they clinked glasses. "Something really worth celebrating." A classic Frank Sinatra song began, and he set down his glass and pulled Dee to her feet. "Finally, something we can dance to again." A few steps took them to the open floor, and he twirled her into his arms, drawing her close, one hand at the small of her back. Pelvis to pelvis, he again began to stir.

Sensing the hardness there, Dee wiggled against it, and, lips brushing his ear, murmured softly, "Look what we've done, Jason."

He chuckled. "Looks like you've awakened someone who wants to help you celebrate, darling." His lips brushed her graceful neck, and then drew in an earlobe inside.

"Oooh, you naughty boy." Her tongue darted against his ear. "We hardly know each other, and already you call me darling."

"It just seemed natural, Dee." He arched back. "You're exactly who I'm looking for." A gentle kiss, tongue barely teasing, was at first not rejected, then soon greeted with warm response. Their lips parted, each panting softly.

"This is more than I expected tonight." She studied his face, then stood back and took his hand, headed back to their table. "I thought I was gonna have to celebrate alone, so you're a pleasant surprise ... handsome *and* a gentleman."

"Why would you be alone after a big win? You'd think the others—"

"Too competitive to share."

"Who? Your associates?"

"No, me." She sighed, finished her drink, and nodded at the barkeep for another. "I tend to be aggressive, and that puts most guys off, and the women can't match up."

"Their loss." Glasses clinked with the newly-arrived drinks. "I'm used to strong women." As she glanced across the room, his drink went into a nearby potted plant, following two others.

"In bed, too, Jason?" Her head now canted toward him, onyx eyebrows arched. "I like to take charge. Set the pace and tempo. Sometimes accused of being domineering." She watched him, her eyes a bit unfocused and words slightly slurred. Four vodka gimlets were taking their toll.

"That's never been a problem for me, darling." *Couldn't be more perfect. No instruction needed for a change.* "I'd love a chance to show you how submissive I can be,"

"I dunno." She played with her empty glass. "We jus' met, and now I've gone 'n got smashed." A soft giggle. "I gotta get home," slumping back on her chair.

"Well, you're certainly in no shape to drive." Drawing her to her feet, he tossed money on the table, and with her purse's strap looped over his forearm and an arm around her waist, he led her wobbling toward the door. "I'll drive you home."

"You will?" She patted his cheek. "Nice man, helped me celebrate." Staggered to a stop, she took his hands. "Then what?" Their eyes locked.

"What? After I get you home?" He caressed a cheek. "That'll be your call, sweetheart. Send me on my way, or take me inside and punish me."

"Oh, yeah. Fun times." She tugged him toward the door.

Outside, under the portico, they were approached by a valet. "You got a ticket?"

"Nope." She drew him to their right. "Found a spot jus' up the street."

"Okay." A troll of her purse brought up a BMW key fob. "You drive a Bimmer?"

"Uh hu." She wobbled along beside him. "Blue G70." A soft groan. "Geez, I'm smashed. Might be too tipsy to be any fun, Jas'n."

"We'll see, babe." A press of the UNLOCK button on the fob ignited blinking lights and a short honk of their quarry, two cars up the block. Jason helped Dee in, fastened her seat belt, gave her a brief kiss, then donning thin leather driving gloves, circled to enter the driver side. He fired up the engine and glanced at the woman, slumped against the door. "Where to, Dee?"

"Jus' say 'home,' with voice command, and it'll come up on the GPS." A soft giggle. "Handy li'l bastard."

"Got it." Jason voiced the command, got the musical woman's voice giving directions, and took off. The screen showed thirty-five minutes en route to her apartment in Coral Gables. Time for Dee to sober up enough to make this work. His breath came in short pants in anticipation.

~~~

Parked in her named slot in the under-building garage, Jason helped her, still wobbly but sobering a bit, to an elevator.

"Floor?"

"Eight," mumbled, leaning against him for support. "We gonna have a drink, and then what?" Watery eyes found his, and she giggled. "Maybe coffee is better, so I can sober up to do this right."

"Yeah?" He grinned. "And what are we gonna do, Dee?"

With a chuckle, she pulled free of his arms. "You're a good boy, Jas, but if you're willin', I'm gonna teach you how to treat a lady. Jus' a little discipline, b'fore you earn a reward." His face trapped between her hands, she delivered a sensuous, tongue-dueling kiss. "I *really* know how to make that reward worthwhile."

"Sounds exciting, Dee. I can hardly wait." *Then you're going to learn some discipline yourself.*

They stumbled into her apartment, kicked the door shut, and merged into a fierce embrace before Dee shoved him back and started delivering orders. Thirty minutes of being submissive, something the man was very talented at, before actual sex.

Dee's eyes bulged in stunned surprise when, receding from her Everest of orgasmic joy, his previously titillating fingers morphed into a deadly vise around her throat, ending an erotic tour of pleasure with her unceremonious
~~~

demise.

A scowl creased his lips as he regarded her lovely but lifeless figure, sprawled across the bed. "Fucking bitches. They're all the same. Take, take, take." He turned toward the kitchen and retrieved a filet knife. "They got no heart, so she doesn't need this one." He placed the point on her left breast and drove it between ribs, clear to the hilt.

"A wicked heart no more."

Ten minutes were spent wiping down the rooms, the used condom flushed, and her body cleansed with a rag soaked in alcohol. No DNA for the cops, just as he'd done, both in real life and fantasy land. Then he exited the unit and descended the emergency stairway to avoid cameras. In her BMW again, he disconnected its GPS tracker and drove to the Glades and a remote site where he'd hidden a Honda motor bike. He'd dump the car there in the swamp. Blond wig, prosthetic nose, and fake eyebrows stripped and bagged went into the saddlebags to be burned later, and any trace DNA left in the car would be corrupted by the wetland he'd discard the car into, if it were ever even discovered.

He'd be long gone by then, off to the next city. He hoped he could resist for a while his need to punish heartless women. Each time he found one, the urge became stronger. So far, no one to his knowledge had tied the previous ten scattered deaths together.

He wanted to keep it that way.

~ 6 ~

Ankles crossed and propped over the corner of his desk, Al Warner reclined on his office chair, reading an After-Action Report from Detective Beck. He'd wrapped up a pretty simple domestic murder, a woman capping her cheating man, two .38's in the chest. Jack Harris rapping on his door drew him out of the report. He waved his top detective in.

"What's up, Jack?"

"Got a homicide in Coral Gables, Boss." He glanced at his Android. "Female attorney, found dead, naked in her apartment."

"Forced entry?" Warner shoved to his feet.

"Dunno for sure. Just two blues on the scene right now, awaiting us." He watched Warner retrieve his shield and Glock .40 from his desk drawer. "You coming? I can take Olvida."

"Nah, I need ta get outta the office for a change," striding for his door. "Sounds like it might be somethin' more'n run-of-the-mill." He headed out, with Harris on his heels. "I'll drive." He paused. "Maybe you should too, Jack, in case we need ta split up.

Harris nodded and beeped his Camaro as Warner slid into his gray Dodge Charger. Harris followed his boss out of the lot. It was a thirty-minute run to Coral Gables, and Harris mentioned that the Hawk and his CSU team were already on the way.

~~~
~~~

There was no problem IDing the address, with two black-and-whites, their strobes flashing, and the black CSU van parked in front of a ten story, upscale apartment building. They headed inside, Harris toting a roll of Crime Scene tape, and took the elevator to the 8th floor. Apartment 806's door was guarded by a street cop, so Warner went inside while Harris ran a cross strip of yellow tape across the doorway, high enough so by ducking down, they could enter.

Warner glanced around at the fancy furnishing: ivory leather sofa and love seat, walnut credenza, 70-inch wall-mounted plasma TV. Everything top end. The vic clearly made some bucks. Sounds from an open door, clearly the bedroom, drew him, and entering, he found Moe Gold, the Hawk, using some sort of high-tech vacuum on the back skin of a naked corpse, sprawled face down on the bed.

The CSU ace noticed Warner and straightened, stepping away from the body. "Been waiting for you, Detective. I know you don't want anything moved before you have a chance to see it." He waved at the doorway. "Video already completed, so we're ready to go."

"So, what do we know, Moe?" Edging closer, he studied the figure. Nice shape and good butt. Probably a gym rat.

"The vic is one Deena Wright. Called in by a Carlton Schmidt, a partner at her law firm. Got worried when he was a no-show at work, and learned she'd hooked up with some guy at happy-hour last night." He nodded at the door. "That young patrol cop's got all the details. He interviewed Schmidt who, when she was AWOL at work, came by, found the door unlocked, and discovered her like this."

"This Schmidt still here?" Warner glanced at the entry.

"Far as I know. Last I saw, he was sprawled on a sofa, which didn't make me happy, in case he's tainted some evidence." Gold shrugged. "Probably okay, as preliminary sweeps show the place pretty well wiped down." He turned toward the body. "Even bathed our vic in alcohol, clearly to clean any DNA." He gathered up the tool he'd been using. "The newest thing. A sterile vac that will gather up the tiniest bits of cells that we can test for DNA." He set it aside. "This perp was pretty careful, so don't know what we'll find."

Warner donned latex gloves, leaned in, and touched her neck. "Lots of bruisin'. COD strangulation seems likely, huh?"

The Hawk glanced at Warner. "Possibly, but let's not rush things, Detective. You're always in such a damned hurry." He took an arm and leg. "In rigor. So, let's turn her over and see what we can find."

A moment later, Deena Wright lay on her back, eyes bulging wide, filled with petechia, a clear sign of asphyxiation. But Warner's eyes flared at something else.

"Look at that, Moe."

"Yes, Detective. Looks like a knife slit. From the size and angle, I'd suspect straight into her heart." His gloved finger probed the opening. "Not the cause of death, I'd think. We'll let the M.E. verify that, but from the lack of blood, this looks post-mortem."

"Damn! Again?" He grabs the Hawk's arm. "Ring a bell, Moe?" Warner waved a hand over the body.

"Huh?"

"Attractive, black-haired, fortyish woman picks up a guy, has sex, is strangled, and *then* he plunges a knife into her heart?"

"Yes, of course." Gold rubbed his Semitic nose. "About two years ago, another woman—"

"Maria Santiago," Warner growled. "Unsolved"

"Yes, I know those rankle you, Al." He studied their victim. "You believe it may be the same perp?"

"Seems too specific an MO ta be coincidental. I thought at the time it mighta been the beginnin' of a new serial nut, but there were no follow-up murders, and it eventually went inta Cold Cases." Warner rubbed his chin. "The only thing different was with Santiago, the knife was left in place."

"Uh hu. If this *is* the same guy, it's a change in modus operandi." He studied Warner. "So, what are you going to do, Detective?"

"Treat it like a second vic and get Santiago back outta Cold Cases." He glanced around. "Maybe we'll find something this time. See if your fancy vac gets us a new lead." He turned toward the door. "Absolutely no stone unturned this time. Let's come up with something to snag this guy." Paused in the doorway, his eyes swept the room and spied the guy, Schmidt, sitting on a sofa, crouched over, face in his hands. *Probably clueless, but I gotta start somewhere.* He waved at Harris, who was prowling the living room, looking for anything out of place.

They converged on the man, but after a half-hour had learned little more than Ms. Wright was a rising star at Wax, Overhauser, and Schmidt, Esq., and she'd just successfully completed a mega-million-dollar lawsuit against three opioid drug makers, and was about to become a partner in the firm.

Were the losers in that suit angry enough to commit murder, or could an associate of the firm be angry enough to kill at being passed over? No known guy in her life, but while unlikely, all would be run down. Warner knew in his gut that this was the same perp as two years ago, and was still pretty sure there was a serial killer component here.

Al Warner's famous "gut" was seldom wrong.

~ 7 ~

Warner shoved into Detective Harris's cubby and planted both palms, stiff-armed, onto his desk. "So, nothing at all on the Wright case, Jack? No DNA, no prints, no fibers? Nothing?"

"The Hawks magic vac *did* pick up a few cells from her body, Boss, but he says they were too corrupted to be much help. Got a little, partial DNA and ran it against the national data base, but it was so incomplete, he got no hits."

"What about the bar on Brickell where she met the guy? They had CCTV cameras."

"Yeah, and we got some shots of the perp, but he pretty much avoided a full view. Wright's building had them too, in the lobby, garage, and the elevator, but again, nothing clear."

"How 'bout her car? She drove a BMW, but it wasn't at the bar or her apartment."

"Right, Boss. Got a BOLO out on it." Harris glanced at his Android. "The bartender said he heard the guy offer to drive her home, so maybe they went in her BMW."

"So, where is it? Might be our best shot at prints or DNA."

Harris shrugged and picked up a sketch. "We're on it, Boss. The Hawk's artist created a composite of what we got, but what little we know is, he was blond, bushy eyebrows, biggish nose, and probably six-feet or six-one."

Warner took the drawing and studied it. "Pretty indistinct. He try the facial rec program?"

"Yeah, no joy there." The wiry detective shrugged. "If he *is* serial, I'm afraid we're back to waiting for the next vic, and hoping he flubs up."

"Not my favorite thing, Jack. Anyhow, keep at it. Maybe somethin' will pop." Warner rubbed his nose. "Ya know, have the Hawk pull what little images we had from the Santiago case, and see if Tech can find any physical similarities. I know we ain't got much there either, but maybe enough to help tie the two together."

"That guy had black hair, Boss. This perp is blond."

"Probably disguises, Detective. Anyway, it's worth a shot." Turning to leave, he said over his shoulder, "I'm checkin' out early. Eva's takin' me to some fancy Italian joint for dinner, and then we're gonna see a play at the Coconut Grove Community Theater."

"A play? You?" Harris chuckled.

"Yeah. Not one of those musicals. It's a murder mystery, and I guess the audience is supposed ta figure out who dunnit." Warner shrugged. "Might be fun, and I can use the distraction." A wave, and he headed for his office to pick up his jacket, gun, and shield.

Maybe just what I need ta clear my head and get me on track with this bastard. He chuckled. *Bet this is a murder I can solve. Too bad it ain't for real.*

~~~

Warner shoved back the small plate, scattered with the remnants of the delicious Tiramisu, leaned back, and patted his belly. The air swam with pleasant aromas of garlic and oregano. "Good stuff." He smiled at Eva. "How'd ya find this place, babe? Coconut Creek ain't exactly your stompin' grounds."

"Google. What else?" She chuckled. "Just searched
~~~

YELP for best rated Italian restaurant, and there was Bistro Italiano." She lay her hand on his. "You enjoyed the veal Parm?"

"My empty plate was all the evidence you need, darlin'. But the side of linguini Bolognaise was so good, I might just order that for an entrée, if we ever find our way back here."

"I'm sure we will," a glance at her watch, "but we should go or we'll be late for the play."

They rose, and she slipped the paid chit into her purse.

Three-and-a-half-hours later, Warner held open the door of his coupe as Eva slid inside. He felt only slightly guilty for hanging his police ID in his windshield while parking in a restricted zone. All the nearby lots were filled, and he didn't want to leave his Dodge with theater's valets. He slipped into the driver side, checked that Eva was buckled in, and leaned over for a brief kiss.

"So?" Her eyebrows arched as she caressed his cheek.

"I enjoyed it more'n I expected." He fired up the engine and pulled out, heading home. "*A Murder Mystery* was an apt title, and I'm guessin' the ending was a surprise for most."

"You suspected the secretary was the culprit, Al? Why?"

"Well, when it was revealed he was sexually abused by his sicko mom, that seemed more a motive, in his deranged mind, for killin' all those women, than the two guys, 'though they did a pretty good job of tossin' in red herrin's." A quick glance in his side-view mirror, and he pulled into the entry lane to I-95."

"I got the impression you thought the detective was a bit much, though." Eva leaned back and closed her eyes.

"Yeah, well, in real life, ya don't get everyone together and go through a laundry list of who didn't do it, until you point the finger." He chuckled. "They were goin' for the big

Agatha Christie reveal. It don't happen that way."

"Not on your watch, huh?"

"*Never* on my watch, babe. I find my guy, he goes down, right then." A head shake and sigh. "No extra drama needed. I wish catchin' this new perp would be so easy."

A mumbled ascent from Eva brough a grin to his lips. She'd had a busy day he knew, especially with three cops suffering from PTSD. Like him, work can take it out of her. Tonight was a good chance for some relief. Warner glanced at his redhead wife, always in awe that this beautiful woman loved him.

Let her rest for the thirty-minute drive home. He had plans to keep her up after they made it into bed. Luckily, she loved making love with him as much as he did with her. Probably after a peach turnover that his adopted "mom," Adele, would have baked while sitting Andrea for them.

His thoughts shifted to his latest murder and wondered if it were time to call in the BAU. If this were the acts of a serial murderer, the FBI wanted in. But, two years apart? That still seemed iffy. A second sigh as he drove on, filled with indecision.

~ 8 ~

Current time, two years later

Marla Anders paused just inside the doorway of the Grove Bistro and scanned the lengthy bar. Shoulder-length, onyx hair swirled as her eyes swept the room, pleased it was so busy, even at eleven-thirty p.m. She spied two couples she'd noticed at the play, and some singles she though may have been part of the cast. She'd gone to see *A Murder Mystery* as an escape from the usual community theater musicals and had enjoyed it more than she'd expected. It was an interesting plot twist at the end, and she'd been delighted at the surprise. The full cast, probably eight to ten men and women, had been quite professional. Too bad Gloria cancelled at the last minute, struck by a severe cold. Not Covid, she'd said, but who needed to catch it, whatever it was. Marla was happy she'd persevered and came alone.

She strolled to the long, epoxy-coated oak bar, and took a stool near the end. "Manhattan," she told the female barista, then swiveled to view the room, looking for company. An attractive redheaded guy was just returning his dance partner to the bar, but his eyes were on her. His lips tilted into a sly grin, and his bushy, auburn eyebrows arched. Tiny electric feet skipped down her spine as Marla returned his smile. He said something to the woman, then sauntered over to where she sat.

"Mind if I join you?" His voice a soft tenor.

"Of course," she nodded down the bar, "but aren't you

occupied?"

"Oh, no." A small head shake. "Just someone I danced with until you arrived." The grin was now whimsical.

"Me?" Her forehead wrinkled. "You were waiting for me? But, I don't—"

"Oh, no," he interrupted and chuckled, "not you, specifically. Just you remind me of someone very important to my life. Physically." He shrugged. "I always have to meet someone like that ... someone who stirs important memories." He took her hand. "I'm Jason," then kissed its back.

Marla giggled. "So gallant. I'm Marla." She turned to the bar, picked up her drink, and took a sip. "So, Jason, what brings you to South Florida? Not your home, I'm guessing."

"Right. I'm here for work for about ten days."

"Oh? What kind of work, if I may be so bold."

"I'm an actor. We're doing a play at the Coconut Grove Community Theater."

"*A Murder Mystery?*"

"Yep. That's it." He took a swig of the Scotch he'd ordered. "Just came over for a drink and to wind down." His eyes swept the room. "Usually, several cast members are here after the show, but it looks like I'm solo tonight

"Oh, I just saw that play this evening." Eyebrows arched, she lay a hand on his. "Really enjoyed it, but I don't remember seeing you on the stage."

"Well, you wouldn't recognize me if I were, because I play the part of the aged accountant," he lied easily, "gray wig and mustache, but I was off this evening." He shrugged. "They were breaking in a new, backup cast member for the part."

"Oh, I see." She sipped her cocktail. "Well, I really enjoyed it. Nice break from all the musicals." Marla gave a small chuckle. "More engaging, when you're trying to figure out who dunnit."

"And did you?"

"Nope. Totally surprised." Again, sampling her drink.

"Well, that's the idea." He took her hand and slipped off his stool. "Gotta keep those cops on their toes." He tugged on her arm. "Finally, something slow. Care to dance?"

"Love to," as she rose, and he led her to the small, impromptu dancefloor.

Twirling her first, he drew her into body-to-body contact, heads nestled cheek-to-cheek. "You smell delicious, Marla. What is that sexy fragrance?"

"Channel No. 5." She chuckled. "Old school, but still a staple." Her heart was doing a tap dance in her breast from the sensuous way their bodies moved against each other. *I didn't expect to get laid tonight, but this guy is so hot.* She swallowed hard. *Let's not rush into things, here.* Marla tried to ease a bit of separation, but his embrace was tight. *What the hell.* She relaxed and flowed with the music.

"So, do you live in the area, Marla?" His smoothly shaven cheek caressed hers, skipping little electric feet down her spine.

"A bit south, in Kendall." She inhaled his musk cologne. "My office is nearby, and I come to the Groove frequently for their upscale shops."

"Your office? What kind of work do you do?"

"I'm a realtor. Grove Realty. Pretty hot market right now." She chuffed. "Elite properties selling for record prices."

"So, that must be pretty exciting." The ballad ended and music morphed into something high-tempo, so Jason led her back to their drinks at the bar.

"You'd think so. Big commissions on sales, but the inventory is low and demand's high, so units go in days, which makes it hard to find something for a client before it's already sold."

"A happy conundrum, I suspect."

She giggled and took a healthy swig of her drink. "I guess. Keeps me on my toes, anyhow."

An hour, four dances, and three drinks later, and Marla found herself at a cozy, corner table, snuggled in Jason's arms, sharing passionate kisses and plenty of touchy/feelie. His hand, under the table, crept under her skirt, a finger patrolling between her thighs, eliciting panted moans of pleasure.

"You're such a naughty boy," whispered into his ear. "I love it."

"You're everything I hoped for tonight, Marla. I can get a hotel room, or go to your place to take this where it needs to go." His kiss was hard and wet. "I've got plans for you that need to be fulfilled." His busy finger brought a quite gasp.

She shivered and grabbed his wrist, withdrawing his hand. Her eyes caught his blues which seemed to be sparkling with a strange intensity. She was in sexual euphoria, but what she saw in his eyes seemed different. Almost maniacal. She shuddered, and struggled for some separation. He wasn't ceding any.

"Jason," she panted. "Give me some space here."

His brow wrinkled. "Geez, babe, I thought we were getting somewhere special." He eased his grip, and they slid slightly apart.

"Yeah, that's the problem." She lay a hand on his arm. "I'm ... I'm just not ready for this. It's all too fast." Marla knuckled her eyes. "Maybe egged on by too many Manhattans." A soft chuckle. "I needed to unwind, so the play, then drinks. Rushing into sex is a bridge too far tonight, though." She stroked his cheek. "You seem like a nice guy, and it woulda probably been great, but I'm just not ready." She edged back and gathered her purse. "I really wanna thank you for a pleasant evening, but I gotta go now. One more drink and I won't make it home alive."

"I can drive you, if you wish. I'm sober." They rose from the table together.

"No. No, that's fine. *I'm* fine, but thanks for the offer. I'm really sorry if this led to less than you'd hoped, but I'm sure you understand."

"Of course. I never force myself where I'm not wanted." He sighed. "I just felt like, this time I *was* wanted, but that's your choice." He took her elbow and started for the exit. "I'll walk you out. Make sure you can find your car."

She shrugged loose from his grip, a slithery chill quickly sobering her. "That's okay. I can find it with no problem. You stay and enjoy your evening." As she made it out the front, Marla glanced back. Jason stood there, watching her, a hand stroking his chin. Then he sauntered her way.

Marla spun trotted, high heels be damned, toward her Lexus sedan. Was that creep following her? She picked up her pace, fumbled for her key fob, and finding it, clicked the UNLOCK button, and then the REMOTE START tab. Inside quickly, tossing her purse on the passenger seat, she locked the door, and didn't wait for her seat to move fully into its automatic position. She pulled away from the curb, almost clipping the car in front of her, and accelerated down the avenue. A glance in the rearview didn't show another vehicle following, but she didn't slow to the speed limit for several blocks.

A sigh was followed by a shiver. Somehow, something that was going so well had turned into something almost scary. Was she paranoid, or was there something suddenly malevolent emanating from that handsome guy? She shook her head, feeling fortunate to be heading home alone that night. She had no idea how lucky she'd been.

~ 9 ~

Warner's eyes swung to his door where he spied ADA Lucita Santamaria rapping on its frame.

"Got a minute, Detective?"

"Sure, counselor. C'mon in." He swept two reports aside and eased back. "This about De la Fuente?"

Nodding, the petite, very curvy blonde attorney perched on the end of his side chair, said, "Yes," and flipped open the file in her grasp. "I just want to be sure we've got it all before we proceed."

Warner grunted. "Offering a plea deal, are ya?"

"Being considered, rather than tie up in the courts and spend taxpayers' money on a lengthy trial." She sat back, eyebrows arched. "So?"

"Well, no doubt he did it." Pawing through a small stack of files, he withdrew one, and scanned it. "Got the weapon with his prints, her blood spatter on his shirt with a DNA match, GSR all over him." Arms folded, he regarded her. "She was cheatin' on him, and he capped her. The only thing not clear is if it was premeditated or impulsive."

"My boss and I agree." She closed her file. "He wants me to get *your* assessment on that."

A chuckle bubbled up from Warner. "Wants me ta let him off the hook, huh?" His file returned to a stack on his desk, Warner straightened. "Frankly, I think he never intended to kill her, but things got outta hand." His eyes held hers. "You wanna offer second degree, huh?"

Santamaria sighed and nodded. "Twenty to forty,

eligible for parole, if he accepts."

"I got no problem with that, counselor." Warner rose. "Makes life easier for everyone, and justice gets done." He shrugged. "I got the feelin' the perp really regretted offin' such a sweet piece ..." Another small chuckle. "Sorry, ma'am. Hope I didn't offend ya?"

"No problem, Detective. I've heard worse, and frankly, my boss really values your input." Rising, she turned toward the door. "I'll pass this along, and I suspect Mr. De la Fuente will grab it."

"Me too," said to her back as she exited.

The other file he'd been reading retrieved, Warner went over it for the umpteenth time. Maria Santiago, and two-years later, Deena Wright: both lingering in Cold Cases now, but never far from Warner's mind.

Unsolved murders haunted him, and these smacked of the product of a serial killer. But, to his knowledge, there'd only been this pair, separated by years. Moe's partial DNA match, vacuumed from Wright, produced no direct hits, but did scare up a file from another attractive, forties, black-haired gal in Atlanta, five years ago, strangled by a guy from a one-night-stand. But, no knife to the heart. It was less than a 20% DNA match, but Warner tried to follow it up. Problem was, the detective on the case retired two years ago and moved to Hawaii. Warner tried to track him down, but so far, no luck. The M.E. at the time had died of a heart attack a year ago, and the current doc was unfamiliar with the case. Said he'd see what he could learn, but Warner wasn't holding his breath. The guy hardly bubbled over with enthusiasm at digging through old files.

Slouched back in his chair, eyes cold, he was running what little he knew through his mind, when his detective, Dean Beck, strode in.

Warner lurched upright and rubbed his eyes. “What’s up, Beck?”

“Three dead in a shootout in Little Havana, Boss.” He hunkered inside the doorway. “Looks like Cubans and Colombians are at war again.”

“Terrif-f-f-ic.” Warner was on his feet, digging for his shield and Glock. “I knew it’s gotten too quiet.” Striding toward the door, Beck already on the move ahead of him. “Where?”

“A bodega near *Calle Ocho* and 22nd,” glancing over his shoulder at his trailing boss. “First report was a soldier from each side, and an innocent bystander.”

“Shit. I *hate* that.” He spied Detectives Harris and Olvida also on the move. “Harris, you drive, and take Salinas. Ralph, hang back in intel. Beck’s with me.” He shook his head. Murder took precedence over cold cases, but he couldn’t get those two attractive, dark-haired vics out of his mind.

They’ll have to wait until he has some free time. A rare damned thing at Miami-Dade Homicide. But then he’ll track down that Atlanta detective, basking in the Hawaiian sun, and see what he can learn. He was sure there was more to it then appeared on the surface.

Right then, he had to put a damper on what were sure to be flaming tempers in the Latin quarter called Little Havana, or they were going to get another full-out gang war.

Not if *he* had anything to say about it. They hit the parking lot on the run, and two cars tore off, sirens blaring, red and blue lights flashing in the grills.

Warner grunted to himself. *Gonna be late again for dinner, but I’ll be damned if I’m gonna miss a piece of Adele’s peach pie.* He chuckled, picturing his ninety-one-year-old neighbor and “adoptive” mom. More Mom than his actual parent had ever been.

He glanced in his rearview, Harris's Camaro close behind. Detective Salinas was a great addition to his team because the Latinos were more apt to open up to one of their own. And, luckily, he was a damned good cop.

He concentrated on driving as Detective Beck rattled off directions. They were only fifteen minutes away.

Cold cases would await another day.

~ 10 ~

The redhead man stepped out of the blue Toyota Crown sedan, parked in front of Room 121 at the La Quinta Inn, located in Miami Springs. He glanced around the nearly empty parking lot and saw no one, so he moved to the door and fished a small electronic fob from his pocket. Tech buddy, Jeremy, guaranteed it would open any electronic lock, and a quick pass over the door's entry plate proved him correct. The door clicked open, and he flipped the safety lock bar around as a wedge to keep it from relocking.

Returning to the passenger door, which was opened, he offered the slightly buzzed black-haired woman his hand to help her out, and gathered her athletic form into his arm for a hug and gentle kiss. "We're here, sweetheart."

"We're where, Jason?" Eyes sweeping the lot, she found the open door. "I thought we were going to your place."

"This *is* my place, darling. Remember, I'm on tour and only here for ten days."

Serena Redding ran long, red-nailed fingers through her straight, silky hair, and laid a hand on his shoulder, gaining her balance. "So, this is gonna be a one-night-stand?" Fingers curled around the back of his neck, she drew their lips together for a more heated kiss. "I was hoping, if it went well—"

"Then we'll have a week to enjoy ourselves, and the cast is scheduled to return in seven months." His arm hooked through hers, grasping her wrist, they moved toward the beckoning doorway. "If you're the stern mistress you promised, this will be something very special."

Her media post on the dating website listed mild domination as an optional feature. Forty and darkly beautiful, she was the perfect prospect, and their hookup at the Miami bar had gone smoothly. So, here they were.

Serena chuckled as her eyes swept the room, which strangely appeared unoccupied. "You're checked in here? It doesn't look used."

"Yeah, just got her and went looking for ... you, I guess. My bags are still unpacked."

"So, you've been a bad boy, looking for discipline, huh? Need me to get you on track?" Fingers caressed his cheek. "Mend your naughty ways, and you'll earn a wonderful reward." She spun the man around and shoved him down, sitting on the bed, and unbuckled and withdrew his belt. "But first a little punishment to make your reward more exciting."

"Oh, yes, ma'am. Teach me to be good, and we'll *both* get our just rewards."

Serena's gaze swept over him, her tongue swiping ruby lips. Something strange the way he said that. Yeah, well bondage wasn't her main thing, but it could be *so* exciting, and this guy was a handsome hunk. She unbuttoned her blouse, displaying a well-filled, sheer lace bra, and edged forward, brandishing his leather belt.

An hour later, the man finished dressing and buckled his belt. His eyes fell on Serena, spread naked across the bed, eyes wide and distended, the result of him strangling her at the height of her orgasm. She thought it was part of their performance together, not realizing it was solely *his* part, not hers. He bent over, lips brushing her still-warm lips, and sighed. He'd really been into the first one ... Marla Anders ...

but Serena proved to be a more than adequate fill-in. Another cold-hearted bitch, willing to watch him suffer.

A shrug and another sigh as he continued wiping down the few things he'd touched in the room. The condom was flushed, carefully avoiding any contact that might leave DNA. Alcohol retrieved from his small back pack was used to wipe down Serena's body, so lovely for a forty-year-old, then he sprayed the bedding and carpet where he'd stood. Not perfect, but sufficient to corrupt any DNA cells that he may have left. There was, to his knowledge, no DNA data base to ID him directly, but he hoped to obscure his connection to what was now fifteen dead, black-haired women.

A survey of the room assured he'd done what he could. So, a five-inch blade folding knife was withdrawn from his bag, and with precision, thrust into her wicked heart. A final look around, and he strode into the bathroom and opened its casement window. A few moments later, he was out the back of the motel, out of sight of any CCTV cameras, hurrying into the back lot of a Seven-Eleven, where he'd parked his rental, again clear of any security cameras. He stripped away the red wig, eyebrows, and small mustache, bagged them for burning later, and relived the excitement of the evening.

He groaned softly and shook his head. He wanted to stop his quest, but instead, he was escalating. So many wicked women needing to be punished.

Needing their wicked hearts purified. He'd become so *good* at finding them.

He snickered as he drove off, any sense of guilt shed. He'd lied to Serena. This tour was over in two days, not ten. They were off to Charleston for a five-day engagement.

Will I find another woman needing to be purified?

Despite his earlier thought, he was eager to see.

~ 11 ~

A 200-yard sprint, with Buff loping at heel, finished Warner's early morning two-mile run. Slowing the last few yards, he trotted up the steps of his Miami Springs townhouse and paused to catch his breath. A glance at his neighbor's door, and he shook his head. Six-thirty was too early to knock, even though Adele, soon to be ninety-two, was an early riser. He'd check on her, as usual, when he left for the office.

Unlocking his door, he entered quietly, but then the aroma of brewing coffee and frying bacon wafted over him. Eva was up and preparing breakfast. He remembered his psychiatrist wife had an early appointment with an Afghanistan vet suffering from PTSD. She'd weaned him away from suicidal thoughts, and for the first time in six years, he was holding down a full-time job as a mechanic at a Mercedes dealership. Warner grinned, continually amazed, even after eight years, that this amazing woman loved *him*.

He entered the kitchen just as she turned from the cooktop with a stack of buttermilk blueberry pancakes, and his gut rumbled in anticipation.

"Ha." She grinned. "Perfect timing." A hand wave directed Buff to his bowl. "Breakfast is ready for everyone." She set the platter on the table beside a beaker of Vermont maple syrup, as the big golden retriever ambled into the corner and emptied half his water bowl, before attacking the tasty, all-natural meal awaiting his attention. A well-mannered pup, he'd lick his bowl clean when finished.

Warner drew his wife into his arms for a lingering kiss, then turned to giggles emanating from his three-year-old daughter, perched in her highchair.

"Daddy loves Mommy," she sang, waving her arms.

"And Mommy loves Daddy, Andrea," Eva said, both turning toward the child.

"And we both love our little Andrea," they voiced together, followed by chuckles. They settled at the table, and Warner forked four fluffy pancakes onto his plate and doused them with syrup, then plucked up three pieces of crisp bacon.

His eyes caught Eva's emerald orbs. "How's the party plannin' goin', babe?" Their neighbor, Adele Gerber, was turning ninety-two at the end of the week, and they were going to celebrate, as they did with Warner's new "mom" every year. Her younger sister, Kira, was arriving from Isreal that evening, and Eva would pick her up at Miami International if Warner was tied up at work. The detective and the Israeli became friends when she, an ex-Mossad operative, had helped him ID an assassin seeking revenge on other Mossad members who'd retired in South Florida.

"All according to plan," Eva said, chewing a small bite of blueberry pancake. "Everyone has RSVPed, and we'll have twelve, which is about the max we can handle here." Dabbing pink lips with a napkin, she rose. "Cake's ordered from Publix." She chuckled. "Won't be as good as one Adele might bake, but I can't ask her to bake for her own party." She picked up the now empty food platter and turned to the sink. "At her insistence, there won't be any gifts, but I still bought a customized apron, with 'The World's Best Mom' embroidered on it." She grinned at her husband, "She'll love that, coming from you."

"Thanks, babe. You're the—" He paused, grunted, and withdrew his vibrating cell phone, glanced at the screen, then clicked the green button. "What's up, Harris?" Brow furrowed, he glanced at Eva and shook his head. "On the way, Jack. Still home, and I gotta shower and change, but I'm only ten minutes away. See ya there in about thirty." He pulled his redhead wife into his arms and kissed her forehead.

"Murder vic in a nearby motel, darlin'. Gotta shower and change. You okay with the imp?"

She nodded. "I always take her with me for this client. For some reason, seeing her playing with dolls and stuff relaxes him." She stepped to the highchair. "Adele wants her later, so all the bases are covered."

"My three favorite women," Warner said as he hurried for their bedroom. "Don't know how I could get through life without 'em, anymore." A quick, hot shower, then clad in khaki cargo slacks, a short-sleeve shirt, and a denim jacket, which covered his holstered pistol, he was out the door and away in his custom Dodge Charger.

Murder never waited for the tardy in Miami, and Warner hated being late to the scene.

~ 12 ~

Warner was familiar with the La Quinta Inn, not five miles from his house, and arrived as promised, exactly thirty-minutes after Harris's call. The inn's parking lot was mostly filled by black-and-whites, unmarked detective cars, the CSU van, and the meat-wagon. He wasn't happy when even the M.E. beat him to a crime scene.

Exiting his Charger, he paused, squinted against the sun, hands on hips, and scanned the lot. Late morning now, and not many vehicles of patrons, so a witness list may be pretty thin. He spied two CCTV security cameras, so maybe they'd have some video of the vic and the perp entering Room 121, the crime scene. A green Nisson showed Detective Beck was already on site, but no sign yet of Harris, who was coming all the way from North Miami.

Warner strode past a lady cop, her blues crisp and on point. She nodded toward the door and mumbled, "Creepy." Inside, Warner found the Hawk examining a corpse on the bed: a woman with silky black hair. Warner's gut tightened, and he muttered, "Shit." Two strides took him to the bed, and he laid a hand on the little CSU whiz's shoulder.

"This what I think it is, Moe?" Lips tightened into a slit as he noted the bruised neck and knife wound on her left breast.

"Yes, Detective. This time, you don't have to remind me." He straightened and turned to Warner. "Another attractive, black-haired woman of about forty, strangled during or just after intercourse, then stabbed, postmortem, in the heart." He shrugged. "Shades of your second serial killer, the Angel of Death. Seduce, screw, then strangle, but those victims were much younger, and there was no knife wound."

"Got an ID?"

"Not yet. No purse or wallet visible." He nodded toward the door. "Your detective is checking the Toyota out front. May be hers."

Warner grunted, and his eyes cast around the room. "This guy leave a message like that other bastard did? 'Vengeance,' scrawled in red on mirrors?"

"We're just getting started scrubbing the scene, but so far, no, except maybe for the knife wound." He grimaced and shook his head. "Three victims now, each about two years apart, but the same MO, except no knife left in the wound here." His eyebrows arched. "What do you think, Al?"

"Well, three makes him serial. Maybe he's someone on the road, like that long-haul-trucker out west." A finger massaged the crease beside his nose. "I'm guessin' there're more dead babes out there, maybe scattered around, and the FBI either hasn't yet tied 'em together, or hasn't alerted us about it."

"Because they're each two-years apart? Maybe that's some sort of timeline for him."

"Sure, that's possible, but in my experience, these guys escalate—speedin' up, not slowin' down."

"So, you going to call in the BAU again, Detective?"

"Probably. This is their area, and I've worked with Special Agent Pauletti's team several time in the past."

"Agent Pauletti's running that team now?"

"Yeah. After the Shadow sniper killed Agent-in-Charge, Ed Dalwin, Pauletti took over." He sighed. "What a deadly bastard that was."

"Not for long, when Detective Al Warner's on their trail." Gold patted his back.

"Yeah." The chuckle was mirthless. "Well, we need this perp to make a mistake before any more bodies pile up." He looked at the Hawk. "You seen Beck?"

"I believe he's questioning the desk clerk, and—"

Just then Detective Dean Beck entered the room. He nodded and joined them.

"Give me something good, Beck," Warner grumbled.

"Nothing useful, Boss. Apparently, no one checked into Room 121. The perp musta had an electronic key scanner to pop the lock." He studied his notes on his Android. "No occupants in any rooms near 121, so no one reported anything."

"Not even their arrival?"

"Nope, but we should see that on the security footage. The clerk's pulling the SD cards now. Good coverage, so we should see them arrive and enter the room."

"The night clerk didn't see someone unregistered showin' up?"

"According to the day guy, he's a college kid studying for a law degree, making a few extra bucks. Doesn't do much more than fill the night seat in case someone needs something." He glanced again at his tablet. "The morning cleaning woman noticed a Do Not Disturb sign on the door but knew the room was unrented, so she peeked inside, found the vic, and reported it to the day guy."

"You question her?" Warner began cruising the room, with Beck tailing.

"No chance, Boss. She told the clerk what she'd found, then took off. I suspect she's undocumented and didn't want talk to cops."

"Too bad. Find her and see if she knows anything."

Warner grunted. “Unlikely, but we’re gonna cover all the bases. We got ourselves another bonified serial nut, so we ain’t gonna take anything for granted.” He paused. “She Latina?”

Beck nodded.

“Take the new guy, Salinas, with ya. She may respond better to one of her own.” He pivoted at a noise from the bathroom and moved to that doorway. One of the Hawk’s techs stood on a toilet, peering out an open window into the motel’s back lot.

“Ya got something, buddy?” Warner asked.

“Looks like the perp might have exited the room through this window.” He waved a hand over the opening. “Big enough for an athletic guy, and I might see some trace on this sill.” One of his team entered the room and handed him a collection kit. He swabbed the sill, frame, and a thumb lock.

“Don’t know how good it’ll be, but it looks like skin cells.” Stepping down, he faced Warner. “Hard rain here last night, so it may be corrupted, but we’ll run it through the lab. See if we can get a match.”

Warner stepped aside to let him pass. “Here’s hopin’.” He reentered the room. “Meanwhile, I think I will call the BAU. See if any of this rings a bell with other cases.” He joined the Hawk, still lingering beside the bed. “Find anything else helpful, Moe?”

“Nothing obvious, Detective. We’ll get the body to the lab for a thorough scan, and then it’ll be up to the M.E.’s autopsy.” He glanced at the figure, still lovely in death, if you didn’t look at her bulging eyes. “Definitely seems the same M.O. as the other two murders, so I’m pretty sure you’re on the right track, with this being serial.”

“Yeah. The strange thing is the two-year intervals. Whatever, Santiago and Wright are comin’ back outta Cold

Cases. Maybe, we'll finally be able to give their families closure." He pivoted on Beck. "You stick here, Dean. Get that surveillance video and see what ya can learn, I'm heading for HQ to call the BAU. Past time we got them involved."

In his Dodge, heading for the city, he dialed a saved number, the cell for Agent Pauletti. Two rings, sounding over his blue-toothed car's speaker, and it was answered.

"Detective Warner." Agent Pauletti's voice filled the car's interior. "Knowing you, I suspect this isn't a social call. What can I do for you?"

"Looks like we got another serial killer, Lon."

"Yes? How many, Detective?"

"Just body-bagging the third, all fortyish, attractive, black-haired women."

"Same M.O., Al?"

"Yeah, each strangled after sex, then stabbed through the heart postmortem, and they each dropped two years apart."

"So, you're saying three over the past four years?" He paused. "You're thinking a traveling killer?"

"Seems likely." Warner turned into HQ's lot but lingered over the blue-tooth connection. "I'm hopin' ya can check Eastern and Midwestern jurisdictions for something similar, and then get down here with your team."

"On it, Detective. FAX me what you have, and we'll be there, ASAP."

"Good." He paused. "Ina Yeager still on your team."

"Yes. All the same agents as last time."

"Good. Be sure that Amazon brings her long gun, Lon."

"You like that? She never leaves home without that Barret .50. Think you'll need it?"

"Just ta be safe. She saved my ass three times with sharp shootin', so ya never know."

They chuckled and disconnected. Warner headed for his

office to gather up what he had and send it to the FBI. After that, it was a waiting game, hoping for clues and leads to catch this perp before he killed again.

Warner dealt with murder every day, but nothing angered him more than someone with a specific agenda, selecting victims to meet his twisted needs.

Those were the bastards that filled his nightmares.

~ 13 ~

The man slouched on a rear seat in the Trailways charter bus, a Red Sox ball cap pulled down covered his nut-brown hair and slitted hazel eyes. His gaze idly swept the seventeen other members of the cast and crew, eating, dozing, or playing with phones. Four hours to the Florida/Georgia border, and they'd be in their Charleston hotel that evening. A grunt followed by a stretch, and he shoved up and plucked his phone from a pocket.

Huddled against the large window, he peered out at the endless orange groves as they sped north. Florida had been good to him—again. A pink tongue swept thin lips as his eyes swept the others, assuring no one was coming to engage him, so he scrolled to his encrypted photo app and entered a password. First photo up was of Serena and he in a selfie, sitting on the bed's edge, nude and grinning. He'd liked that she wasn't at all self-conscious about posing, and looked eager to begin his punishment. The next three were of her in various positions after she'd paid the price for not protecting him. She was a beauty in death, the spitting image of his heartless mom.

Mom, personified.

Mom, needing to be punished for her inaction.

Mom, for letting it happen, again and again, for all those years and doing nothing.

Mom, making excuses, telling him how much they loved him.

Mom, Mom, Mom—more guilty than Dad, because she

was afraid to intervene.

He was only a kid, and ...

Memories were broken by the lurch of the bus and hiss of air brakes as it left I-95 and pulled into a rest stop. Time to stretch their legs, take a piss, and maybe buy some snacks. His phone closed and pocketed, he shook his head as he rose, struggling to quell the surge of obsession coursing through him—the *need* to rebuke mom.

So soon? In Charleston, again? It'd been two years since he last punished a woman there. What the hell was her name ... that faux mom? Jaw clenched, he'd think about it later. Now he needed to take a whiz.

Why can't they hire a bus with a john?

Back on the road, thirty-minutes later, again alone at the bus's rear, he struggled with a losing battle not to dwell. *Fuck it!* His phone back in hand, he opened the encrypted file and scrolled idly through its extensive contents until he found her, the other woman in Charleston. Barb, he remembered, in a lovely, third-floor loft in Olde Towne, overlooking the harbor. A sweet place for love and punishment. A proper place to pay the price.

He studied her photos—trim; perky, augmented breasts; silky onyx hair; and ruby, cupid-bow lips. He massaged his chin, lost in memory. She was the fourteenth who paid the price for not protecting him. He'd thought maybe she'd be the last, but now Serena, that guilty, black-haired bitch, was the eighteenth, and still he knew he wasn't finished. He reveled in those moments of retribution, and was racked with angst afterward. He *knew* these women were *not* his heartless mom. She was long gone, right with his father. Barely out of his teens, he'd seen to both of them, nearly twenty years ago. But, Mom or not, they were all heartless women who did nothing to stop abuse.

Somehow, he'd controlled the persistent need to still punish her, before finally succumbing to that urge after ten years of struggle.

Christine. He scrolled though his phone until he found her photos. His first of two in northern Atlanta. She'd made it too hard to resist, a classic domination lover who paid his mom's debts. A heartless bitch. They *all* were.

He shuddered and closed the app, pocketing the phone, angry at the stirring in his pants these memories always ignited. They'd be in Charleston for five days before moving on to Roanoke. Hopefully, there will be no one in either city to tempt him again. Not likely. There was *always* someone. He sighed.

In his heart he knew he was playing a dangerous game, and the more often he participated, the more likely he'd get caught.

He was unsure if he feared that, or *longed* for it.

~ 14 ~

Al Warner rose from behind his office desk and strode toward his door. A mild clamor in the bullpen indicated the arrival of the BAU's six-person team. No question they were dealing now with a serial killer, and this crack FBI team had been invaluable in tracking down six previous psychos. These were good folks to work with, and unlike many Feds, they didn't try to take over the investigation. They were great profilers, tops at investigating crime scenes, and Ina Yeager's sharpshooting skill was often an asset.

Warner entered the squad room and spied the six Feds getting warm welcomes from Detectives Harris and Olvida. Special Agent in Charge, Lon Pauletti, turned at his approach and offered his hand.

"Agent Pauletti." They shook. "Glad ya could make it so quick." A nod toward Jack Harris. "Harris'll get ya set up in a conference room, and I've got what little we've dug up. Gonna need some work at your end to see if we can tie this into anything else." He gestured at Detective Olvida.

"Olvida's got what we know of the possible five-year-old Atlanta tie-in, but it's pretty thin at this point." He paused, eyes scanning the rest of the team and sighed. "Still seems kinda strange without Agent Dalwin. What's it been, Lon? Four years?"

"Nearly five, Al." He patted Warner's shoulder. "You're not still blaming yourself that he died working the Shadow case with you?" He shook his head. "Could have been a lot more dead at the end with that deadly shooter, but ...?"

"Yeah, an apparent code about not offin' law enforcement. At least we finally got the killer." He shrugged. "Anyhow, we got what seems pretty sure to be a new psycho, leaving a really weird signature, so I'm surprised he hasn't turned up on your radar."

They walked together, the other five BAU members and his two detectives trailing, toward Conference Room One. "With each case years apart and in scattered locales, if we don't get reports from local PD's, it's unlikely we'd make the connection." He gave a friendly shoulder bump. "It took my favorite detective to tie it together. The Miami field office is running a nationwide search as we speak." They settled around the oval oak conference table, and Warner slid over his file. A very thin file.

"The post-mortem knife into the heart should stand out, Lon, don't ya think?"

"Yes, unless that's a newer twist. We're searching strangulation deaths of fortyish, black-haired women, concentrating on the eastern half of the country." He flipped open and began scanning Warner's file. "Should have something by tomorrow, if there is any pattern."

"Especially if there're more'n one, separated by a year or two, in the same locale." Warner eased back in his chair. "That ties inta our preliminary theory of a travelin' killer."

"Right." A sheet was drawn from the folder. "I see a partial DNA match with the Atlanta victim, but no knife wound."

"Yeah. Could be he's escalatin'." He sighed. "Hard ta get much useful in an unsolved case, with the cop retired in Hawaii and the M.E. dead. I hoped your guys could track down the detective and see what he knows."

"On it, Detective." He handed the sheet to Agent Solto. "See what you can dig up on the guy in Honolulu, Anita. We can fly him in, if you see any value in that."

"Copy, Boss." She grinned at Warner. "Always a pleasure to work with you, Detective. Never had a cop who made our job easier."

"Back at ya, Agent." His eyes found the tall blonde Amazon, still standing behind the stocky Latina. "Hope we don't need your sharp eye again, Ina, but Lon said ya brought your Barret .50."

"Never leave home without it, Detective." A smile creased her lips. "I'm making a career outta saving your skin." They all chuckled, and he nodded.

"Hope we don't gotta worry about that this time." He rose. "Okay. I'm gonna leave you guys ta do your thing. Don't know if ya got enough for a profile yet, but whoever this guy is, he's got some serious issues." He glanced around. "I'm guessin' he's moved on to whatever next city is on his radar. I'm hopin' ya can find a pattern and snare him before he comes back ta Miami. I don't wanna bag a fourth body here."

Warner left the room and headed for his office, not confident any real progress would be made. He'd been there before, always forced to await the next victim, hoping the perp made an error that led to his downfall. It wasn't a scenario he liked, and with the likelihood this was a traveling nut job, that might not be for a while.

Meanwhile, he had other current cases to deal with, and detectives to assign to them. Strangled dark-haired women would take a back burner to murders they could actually solve now.

At least until some viable lead turned up.

~ 15 ~

The director and producer joined their eight cast members on the stage for a final bow. A hearty round of applause accompanied the drop of the curtain as the ten people milled around muttering congratulations to each other for another city completed. The play, *A Murder Mystery,* was in its ninth year of touring, and much of the cast and support staff had remained unchanged. This was their third tour to Charleston, and they had two days to relax before they were off to Roanoke for a third appearance there. After that, they had sixteen weeks free before beginning their tenth tour of the South and Southeast.

For the first time in nearly five years, there were going to be some major cast changes. Two of their supporting actors had snagged roles on a new Broadway show and a chance to move into the big time. And their stalworth Inn Keeper was packing it in after finishing this tour in Roanoke, retiring to Idaho to spend his days fly-fishing for trout. Three new people would join them in Atlanta in four months for the start of their new tour, and they'd been forwarded their scripts so they would be properly prepared. While this was an off-Broadway operation, both the director and producer demanded excellence.

Clive Warwick, who played Detective Chalmers, said, "I've reserved a small, private room at Murray's Pub on East Bay Street for a well-deserved good-bye party. Drinks and snacks before we all take off to do our own thing before our final gig in Roanoke." His eyes swept the group, all nodding.

"I suspect everyone will be eager to boogie after our final act there, so we'll say adios now."

"Since we're losing two of our long times friends and co-workers to the Big Time after next week's stop," Travis Mott, a co-lead pitched in, "Clive and I thought that would be a good time to celebrate Nick and Tony for directing and producing such a successful and long running show," to a round of applause and some friendly back-slapping.

"With Josh and Caroline leaving, this makes five that talented duet have promoted to Broadway," Clive continued. "I've had two offers myself, but I prefer this small group, traveling from town to town, performing in intimate, local theaters. Forty-second Street is a daily grind, and everything seems to be musicals nowadays." An arm around Director D'Amato's shoulder for a gentle hug, he said, "This is my family ... my *only* family, and there's nowhere I'd rather be."

"So," Travis said, "we've got the room at Murry's 'til Midnight. Then we're all free to do our own thing. "Sleep in in the morning, do some sightseeing, and I hear the redfish are biting in the bay. Two days free and clear before we catch an early a.m. bus to Roanoke." A wave of his hand. "After that, sixteen weeks to recoup, maybe visit family, or just relax and have fun."

Nick D'Amato clapped his hand for attention from the dispersing group. "For any not coming tonight, remember, after Roanoke, seventeen weeks from Monday in the Atlanta Hilton to prepare for the next tour."

Waved hands and acknowledging grunts were his response. Everyone was ready for the coming break after eighteen weeks on the road.

"See y'all soon," Tony Ryder said and turned to leave, then Warwick grabbed his sleeve.

"You've interviewed these three new guys, Tony?"

"Yeah. One's more experienced than the other two, but

I think they'll fit in. The guy, Edwards, should be perfect for the Inn Keeper, and we'll put the other two into minor roles and move Mark and Wes up to replace the ones who are moving to Broadway." He chuckled. "Don't sweat it, Clive. You'll make 'em onto stars, if I know you."

"Yeah. Well, thanks for the props. I'll tell Mark and Wes to bone up on their new parts after we wind it up in Roanoke."

"They're ready, pal. They'll be happy as clams." With a pat on his friend's back, both men departed the small theater, heading for rental cars and a quick visit to the hotel to freshen up.

He slouched on a stool, back to the bar, his elbows resting on the epoxied oak surface, and scanned the room. A sly finger snuck under the edge of his auburn wig to scratch an itch. The redhead disguise hadn't been used for three previous tour stops, and never in Charleston, so he was at ease.

He sighed as his eyes continued to sweep the room. It was well after midnight since they'd dragged out the after-show party, and the lounge wasn't very busy that Sunday night. Two attractive blondes lingering at the far end of the bar were sipping martinis and eyeing him, but they weren't who he was looking for. A shake of his head, and he swiveled back to the red-oak bar and took a swig of his Scotch, diluted now by melted ice. A soft chuckle rumbled in his chest. He was actually relieved, he realized, not to have found her there that evening. His quest to still that evil heart was becoming reckless. He *knew* none of them were his heartless mother, the bitch who fostered so much abuse on him. That he finally took control—got retribution—never dulled the ache.

They were all cut from the same mold—same look, same hair, same wicked hearts. All ready to punish him. Something they soon regretted. They'd never abuse a boy again, after he was finished with them. But there were so many out there. Could he really stop them all? Should he even still be trying, after all these years?

He stumbled from his thought at the touch of a hand on his shoulder. Wide blue eyes caught his as he turned, and both blondes stood there, smiling and effusing delicious odors of exotic perfumes.

"Oh, sorry if I startled you," said the owner of those lovely orbs. "You seemed ... lonely over here, so we thought you might like some company." Her lips arched into a warm smile, and she settled on the stool to his left. "I'm Cassie, and this is my friend, Lola."

Swiveling on his stool, he eyed each girl and nodded. "I'm Jason, and I've gotta say, I've never seen two more lovely women with such beautiful eyes—emerald green and sapphire blue." A soft chuckle.

"Interesting take," Lola said, a grin twitching her lips. "Not the first thing most guys see when the look at us."

"Well, yeah." He took a hand of each girl in one of his. "You both have great, erotic bodies, if I may be so bold, but I find I can learn a lot more about a woman through her eyes." A waved hand drew over the barkeep. "Can I buy you ladies a refill?"

"That's a good start," said Cassie as she slid onto the adjoining stool and hoisted her glass. "Dirty vodka martinis. Grey Goose preferred."

"Johnie Walker Black for me, on the rocks," Jason said. He glanced from one woman to the other. Blondes, late twenties, gym-rat bodies with great racks that may even be natural. No sense of evil hearts there, either. Women to be appreciated and made love to, not punished. Something he'd gotten away from in his obsessive hunt for wicked hearts. There were no candidates for punishment that evening, so, if this led to a night of pleasure, why not? With both of them? That was intriguing.

"So, ladies, are we gonna have some fun tonight?" Slipping off his stool, he drew both of them onto their feet. "There are two of you. How will I know where to begin?"

"You up for a threesome, handsome?" Lola's fingers caressed his cheek, her thumb lightly swiping his lips. "Cassie and I love to share."

A chuckle bubbled from Jason's lips. "How could a guy say no to that, gorgeous?" Her hand in his, he spun Lola into his arms, and swayed with her to the piped-in music. "Let's dance," as he drew her onto the open floor.

Nice. A beautiful woman to make love to. Two, actually, and no evil hearts to punish. I'll leave that for Roanoke. Cheek to cheek, they moved to the music, and Cassie joined them, drawn in with his other arm.

He was strangely at peace for the first time in many months.

~ 16 ~

Warner tilted back in his chair, ankles crossed, dangling over the corner of his desk. Fingers interlocked across his six-pack abs, this was his "Zen" position while his mind free-wheeled through a myriad of facts and details. The Redding murder, now the third over the past four years, was at the center of his thoughts. No question now they had a serial killer, probably someone who traveled for business, killing victims along the way for some warped, obscure obsession.

Were there other victims, scattered across the South and Southeast, that hadn't yet come to the attention of the FBI? The one in Atlanta, despite absent the knife to the heart, seemed likely. Everything else about her fit the victim profile.

Warner dropped his feet to the floor and reached for the Redding file. Flipped open, he found the second page. Harris discovered, while unscrambling the vic's social media presence, that the woman had a web page featuring the practice of erotic submission.

"Harris," he bellowed.

A moment later, his number one detective materialized at his door. "We got an intercom, you know, Boss."

"Yeah, yeah, I know." Waving him in, Warner handed Harris the page. "Accordin' ta this, Redding practiced domination. You check to see who mighta called her that night, or maybe the day before?"

"Tech's scrubbing her site's history. Didn't seem like a lot there, but I'll have it for you in an hour, Boss."

"Good. I gotta feelin' this submissive sex thing may be connected." He replaced the paper in its file. "What's with the BAU? Pauletti's still in the conference room, but I see Agents Ashkin and Swift are missin'."

"Yeah, they're visiting the crime scene and are going to reinterview witnesses." He peeked at his Android. "Olvida's found the missing cleaning lady, and he and Salinas are on the way to question her, but I don't expect much there. She came on in the morning, and Redding and the perp were there the evening before." Harris rose from the chair. "Anything else, Boss?"

"Yeah." Warner grabbed the stack of files on the side of his desk and did a quick sort through. "Somethin' that's been naggin' at me just clicked." He extracted a folder and flipped it open. "I noticed—" He paused, eyes to his door as Detective Beck burst in.

"What's up, Dean?"

"You know about the rash of high-end carjacking lately, Boss?"

"Yeah, but that's not our—"

"It is now. A classic Jag V-12 coupe was just jacked in Coconut Grove, but this time the driver was killed." He shook his head. "Right out in broad daylight, just as the guy was leaving a fancy lunch."

"In our lap now, then." Warner gathered up his shield and Glock. "I'm gonna give Agent Pauletti a heads-up, and then we'll rumble. Maybe get Agent Yeager ta join us, if she's not hot on a new lead for the serial killer." Hurrying out the door, he shot back over his shoulder. "We'd better drive separately, if she comes."

"On it, Boss. I'll text you the address and get started." He headed for the stairs.

Five minutes later, Warner and Special Agent Ina Yeager were in his Dodge coupe, speeding south toward a new crime scene. Besides able to hit a silver dollar at a thousand yards with her Barret sniper rifle, she was a great crime scene investigator.

Two hours later, Warner, Detective Beck, and Agent Yeager paused outside the entry to Bon Bon Café, eyes shaded against the glare of the westering Sun, gazing at tire burn marks where the classic Jaguar E-type V-12 had peeled off, leaving its owner dead at the curb. Their only moderately viable witness, the restaurant's valet, had very little to offer. He'd delivered the Jag to the curb and was looking inside the bistro at another exiting customer, and only turned, alerted by the soft pop of a probably silenced weapon, in time to see the victim hit the ground. The Latino kid ducked behind his small podium when what he thought was a black guy waved a gun at him before jumping into the coupe and speeding off. He wasn't even sure of the perp's ethnicity because a black ski mask covered his face, but he glimpsed what he thought were black hands. Might have been gloves.

No one inside heard or saw anything. The victim, Howard Pomerance, was there to meet a "business associate," but from the woman's reaction, Warner suspected it was more an affair of the heart. Mrs. Leenie Cordova, who luckily was trailing behind Pomerance, was definitely broken up. Agent Yeager got her into a private room, and woman-to-woman, learned both were married to others, and their so-called business connection seemed very thin. Warner already had Harris digging into both backgrounds, in case this was something other than a carjacking, like an angry spouse. An African-American perp could just as easily be a hired killer. A silenced handgun was a preplanned occurrence, not an unfortunate byproduct of a resisted jacking.

"What d'ya think, Ina? They were cheatin' lovers?"

"Seems likely, Detective. Really couldn't get much out of her, though."

"Well, Harris'll turn over the stones, but the heist tracks with the spate of jackin's that's been goin' on lately. We'll follow both tracks fer now." He pivoted to his detective. "Got anything else, Dean?"

"Not much, Boss." He glanced at his notepad. "No one inside heard anything until the Jag burned rubber. The valet was too busy keeping his head down to see much." He pocketed his notes. "Already an APB out on the car, but—"

"Yeah," Warner cut in. "Either already in a chop shop or gettin' repainted and ready ta ship outta country. They love that fancy, classic sport car in Europe and South America." He turned toward his own coupe, nestled at the curb.

"C'mon, Ina. We'll head back." They climbed in. "Beck can handle things here, and we got a serial killer ta nail, hopefully before we fill any more body bags."

"Sorry I couldn't be more help, Detective."

"Well, ya probably got more from the vic's woman than I mighta, so that's a start." He fired up the engine and pulled out. "Beck and Detective Salinas will work this one. I ain't gonna take this lightly, 'cause this is an escalation." He grunted. "Bad enough ta jack people's car, but what appears ta be calculated murder in the process is pushin' it too far."

"Yes, I know these are the kinds of cases that get under your skin, Al."

"Yeah, I guess." A shrug and a sigh. "We see a lot of murder done in the heat of the moment, or maybe gang-related, but when it's some psycho, like the guy we're chasin', or the result of deliberate planning, well, that's pure evil." His lips pressed into the thin line of a grimace.

"Evil and me just don't get along."

They continued on in silence, heading back to HQ and what little currently awaited them there. Probably not even enough yet for the BAU team to construct a profile of why some nut was killing fortyish, black-haired women, and then piercing their hearts, postmortem.

It would all come, in time. Unfortunately, that may also result in new victims.

He hated that.

~ 17 ~

Warner hunkered over Harris's desk, scanning the detective's plasma screen over his shoulder. He brushed aside a napkin littered with remnants of a chocolate donut and gestured at the street images of a brown Jaguar E-12 coupe turning onto a side street.

"That's the car, Jack?"

"Yeah, Boss." Harris tossed aside a now empty paper coffee cup. "But we lose it down that street. No traffic cams there."

"Where's it lead? Looks industrial."

"Mostly shops and a lot of storage buildings, any of which could be a chop shop. Cut her up for parts, or repaint and ship it outta the country. It's apparently a hot commodity in Europe. Racing Blue seems to be the preferred color."

Warner grunted. "They haven't made this model since the 70's, right?"

Harris nodded. "I think 1974 was the last year. This one was a '72." He stretched his neck, and peeked back at Warner. "Beck's on the way down there, looking for CCTV security cameras that may give us more, and –"

Concentration interrupted by Detective Olvida barging into Harris's cubby, Warner pivoted. "What's up?"

"Drive-by shooting in Overtown, Boss. First report, two kids dead, three adults wounded."

"Shit! Gang related, Ralph?"

"Don't know yet, Boss. Street patrol's on site, controlling

the crowd, but I hear it's gotten pretty rowdy."

"Okay." He turned to Harris. "You and Beck stick with the Jag. See if ya can find their workshop." Back to Detective Olvida. "Mounted up and start over there. I'm gonna see if Special Agent Swift will join us," he said, heading out the doorway. "He's good at crime scenes, and we may get better response from locals to one of their own. Text me the address and we'll meet ya there."

"On it, Boss." He hurried back to his desk for his badge and gun.

"I'll update Pauletti's team, Jack," Warner said over his shoulder as he hurried away, "and keep me posted if ya find anything valuable."

"Yeah, Boss."

A moment later, Warner pushed into the conference room where the BAU had made a makeshift HQ, drawing Agent Lon Pauletti's glance.

"Harris is workin' street cams and CCTVs for our carjackin'. We got bubkus on our serial guy." His eyes found the slim, African-American agent. "Can I borrow agent Swift. We got a drive-by with 2 kids dead in Overtown, and I think he could be a big help gettin' cooperation from the locals."

Pauletti looked at his agent. "L-Shawn?"

"Glad to help, Detective." He rose. "Be good to get on the streets for a bit."

"Okay. Go to it." Back to Warner, Pauletti said, "We're working on a profile for our serial guy, Al. May be a bit skimpy, and we don't even know if he's still around, but it'll be a start."

"Great. I'll set up a conference for all the local departments when I get back." He pivoted toward the door. "Don't know when that'll be, dependin' on what we can learn today. These need quick action, or they tend ta disappear."

He clapped Swift on the shoulder as they exited. “C’mon, Agent, I’ll get my stuff and we’ll boogie.”

“Okay, Detective. I’ll meet you at the door. I presume you’re driving.”

“Who else?” he chuckled. “My Charger has carried me through a lotta tough spots. Don’t leave home without her.”

“So I’ve heard, mostly from Ina.”

“Yeah, my guardian angel. Her and her big gun.” A quick wave, and they split up to retrieve weapons and IDs.

Thirty-minutes later, Warner slid his Gray Dodge under the yellow crime scene tape and parked next to Olvida’s blue Chevy. He spied his detective surrounded by a small crowd, men and women, all appearing quite angry. The M.E.’s black meat wagon was on site, but CSU hadn’t yet arrived. Two red EMT ambulances were loading up a man and a woman on stretchers, while a teenage boy and a mid-twenties man, all black, were being treated for minor wounds.

Approaching the agitated crowd, Warner spied the two victims, laying side by side, covered with tattered blankets. Olvida grabbed the sleeve of the angriest guy, six-foot, beer belly, and full black beard laced with streaks of gray. A Dolphin’s ball cap was pulled low over moist, coal-black eyes. The detective turned the man toward Warner.

“Look. Here’s the Chief of Detectives, Al Warner.” He gave a small yank on the man’s arm. “You think he’d be here if we didn’t think this was important, Omar?” He faced his boss. “They’re worried because this is, as he put it, “Niggers killing Niggers,” that we aren’t gonna put any time into this, Boss.”

“Well, yer wrong, friend.” Warner glanced at the two bodies. “Damned wrong. Nothin’ I hate more’n seein’ two innocent kids killed for no reason. We’re gonna hunt these bastards down, and do it quick. Are you and yer people willin' to cooperate?" He drew agent Swift alongside. "I even brought a crack FBI agent with me, who happened to be here on another case. He's as eager to help as I am." A glance at the man. "Special Agent L'Shawn Swift."

"Let me tell you," Swift said, "you got the best cop in Florida—maybe the best one *anywhere*—on this. No one I'd rather work with. A couple years back, he rescued my sister from sex traffickers, out in the 'Glades."

This met with murmurs and nods, quieting the crowd. Someone muttered, "I heard o' him. He done caught all them serial killer types and shut down that big dope ring, few years ago." Grumbling pretty much gone, Warner had everyone's attention.

Warner stepped over, knelt between the two bodies, the air rank with the scent of blood and spilled bowels, and uncovered their faces. "Shit, they ain't even teenagers."

"Eleven-year-old Enna, and thirteen-year-old Jesus," a slim, thirties woman moaned. "Good kids, workin' hard at school, tryin' ta get outta this cesspool someday." Tears rolled across nut-brown cheeks. "Now look at 'em."

"They is gonna get outta here, Em." Another, older woman wrapped her arm around her. "Jest not like we hoped."

Warner rose as the M.E. approached. "Is this where they fell? Or did someone move 'em?"

"It's where Jesus fell," the bearded man, who seemed like their leader, said. "We moved Enna next ta him. Seemed kinda nicer, puttin' 'em together." He stroked his beard. "Was that wrong?

"It's okay. Nice gesture." A pat on the man's shoulder. "You just show the CSU guys where it happened, and they'll take it from there." His eyes swept the crowd. "Believe me, folks, we wanna catch these bastards as much as you, but we can only do that if ya tell us what ya seen. I know sometimes it's hard ta give up one of yer own, but these guys had no problems killin' yer kids. They're probably laughin' and havin' a beer right now." Arms folded, he studied their eyes, all focused on him. "My detective, and Special Agent Swift, are both ready ta take statements from anyone who can help us nab these heartless baby killers. With yer help, we start puttin' these bastards away, and the killin' will stop, once they know the community is gonna stand up against 'em. What d'ya say?"

This was met with a loud grumble and a surge of people, surrounding the two detectives and the agent. Looked like two more senseless killings of kids were their final straws.

Two hours later, Omar hunkered in the passenger seat of Warner's Charger, followed by Olvida's Caprice, with Agent Swift as company, then two black-and whites, trailing. No sirens or flashing lights to announce their arrival.

"That's it." Bearded Omar thrust a finger toward a tan, peeling, CBS shotgun ranch house behind a broken chain-link fence. A black Chevy SUV sat on the drive, under a carport. "That's the car, too," the clearly angry man muttered, as he reached for the door handle.

Warner grabbed his arm. "Hang on. We're gonna drive right by and then get set up. And *you're* gonna stay right here, in that seat. Move, and I'll book ya for interferin' with an arrest." He squeezed his arm. "I don't want ya gettin' shot, this goes sidewise." He glanced in his rearview. "We got plenty of back up."

Warner keyed his cell, answered on the first ring. "Ya got the warrant, Ralph?"

"Yeah, Boss. Just got the text, and they're Faxing a hard copy. Ah," a whirring sound, "here it comes. All legal and ready to go."

"Okay. You and Agent Swift take one of the patrol units and cover the back. Full vests for everyone, ya hear? I'm bettin' they got no idea we'd be on 'em so quick, but they still got guns."

"Gotcha, Boss. No one's gonna take any unnecessary chances. You don't think they're gonna want to come quietly, huh?"

"Maybe not. And if they open up, I don't want any heroics, like trying ta wound 'em. They shoot first, you shoot ta kill. I ain't losing any of my guys here today. Tell the patrol boys, too."

"On it, Boss."

"Good. Beep me when yer set up in back. I'll wait a few ta see if SWAT shows, but we'll go it alone if we hafta."

"Whenever you're ready, Boss. No one does this better'n you. We're gonna circle now into the alley. Should be two minutes, max." And he disconnected.

Parked on the grassless swale, Warner exited his coupe and signaled the two officers in the black-and white to do the same. Heat waves radiated from the pavement, the air rife with garbage from a nearby dumpster

"Vest up," said softly, "and weapons ready. A few spare mags would be good." He spied something through their windshield. "One of ya should take that 12-gauge Mossberg and a pocket full of shells. Good tool in close quarters."

They nodded, slipping on Kevlar vests, and the taller cop retrieved the pump-action shotgun and checked it was loaded and ready to go.

Warner returned to his car and tapped on the passenger window, which spooled down. "Stay put, ya hear. This should be over in a couple of minutes. Hopefully, we get 'em all in one shot, and maybe you guys'll have some peace up there for a while."

The big man sighed and nodded. "I jest wanna see these bums go down." His eyes caught Warner's. "No one in my neighborhood would hold it against you if'n they died here, Detective."

"I gotcha, buddy, but our job is ta catch 'em. Let the courts mete out punishment. But it'll be what it'll be. It's gonna be up to the perps to decide to live or die." A twirled finger led to closing the window, and Warner turned to his companions as his phone peeped. "Okays, guys, we're on." He stepped through the hanging askew gate. "Let's do this."

Warner and one of the officers bracketed the door, and the third stood back, brandishing the shotgun. A gentle turn of the handle found it unlocked. Warner eased it ajar, then shouted, "Miami Police! We have a warrant. Open up, or we're comin' in."

Grunts erupted inside, chairs scraping across wood floors, and the familiar "clack-clack" of a ratcheting gun barrel slide. No one said a word, so Warner kicked open the door and dove in low. The crack of two shots going over his head was quickly followed by the double roar of his officer's 12-gauge. Warner spied three black men, crouching, semi-automatic handguns belching flames. Despite his earlier admonitions, a .40-caliber slug from his gun took one guy in the left shoulder, just as Olvida, Swift, and the other two cops burst through the back door. The other two perps looked at each other, then dropped their weapons and raised their arms, the air awash with the scent of gunfire and the coppery odor of spilled blood. The patrol officers quickly cuffed their arms behind their backs and hauled them out the door. Warner dialed for a bus for the wounded guy, then cuffed him and stuffed a cloth into the wound to staunch the blood. He'd live.

Two-hours later, the house taped off, CSU had done the preliminary sweep and bagged the weapons for ballistic matches for slugs recovered at the drive-by. It looked like they had plenty enough to convict, and the two uninjured thugs were competing to see who could rat out who, first. A jury would decide which to convict of first-degree murder, with special circumstances, which would get them the needle. The State of Florida had no compunction completing the death penalty, and good riddance, as far as Waren was concerned. He did what he did because he hated senseless killing, and had a special passion for killers of children and helpless women.

With this one tied up in a neat bow, all in one day, he had time to return to HQ and see what turned up on their carjacking killer. With the FBI's enhance programs borrowed, he hoped various traffic cams and CCTVs would show them the way to those perps too. He'd love to tie that one up, so he could get back to chasing a killer of attractive, black-haired, fortyish women.

Unfortunately, nothing new had turned up. Pauletti's team was working on a profile, which they'd deliver to the local troops, hopefully within a day or two. He detested that their likely best chance would be another victim and the killer making a mistake. But, with a traveling perp, that may be a while. If things bogged down, the BAU team would leave, because they'd surely have other case to work on. It was a waiting game, something Warner hadbeen forced to do before, but it never got easier.

It was after seven p.m. when Warner finally trudged through his townhouse's front door, after a brief visit to his neighbor, Adele, to see if she needed anything. She'd just finished baking a cinnamon apple raisin pie and invited he, Eva, and the baby over after dinner for coffee a slice, his second favorite way to end his day.

Little Andrea was probably napping, so he planned on

partaking in his *first* most favorite way by making slow, passionate love to that gorgeous redhead who awaited him at home. Then, some play on the floor with his miracle baby girl, a brief run with Buff, his rescued and very loyal golden retriever, then dinner and some pie.

He chuckled, picturing Buff guarding their door while they were involved in bed. The dog took that responsibility on his own, after Eva's near death at the hands of that vengeful assassin. Buff's fierce attack had delayed it long enough for Warner to make a deadly rescue.

He found Eva in the kitchen, just finishing her pasta meat sauce, one of Warner's favorites. Redhair flouncy, she looked fetching in her flowered, pink apron, he took her in his arms and turned off the stove. No words were needed. With the bedroom door closed and the baby asleep, they slipped off their clothes as he heard Buff settle on the floor outside.

The world, at least for that moment, had returned to normal, if you could call making love to the most fabulous woman in the world, normal. For him, it was Nirvana.

~ 18 ~

Warner tilted forward, forearms atop his desk, eyes darting between Agent Pauletti and Agent Yeager. The scrape of chairs and ringing phones from the bullpen seeped past the closed door.

"So, still nothing from your end?"

Pauletti shook his head. "Not yet, but we're working on it." He shifted on his seat. "Miami Field Office has our best algorithms for this kind of search."

"Unsolved cases of fortyish, black-hair women, strangled during a tryst?"

"Yes," Yeager pitched in, "with or without the telltale knife wound, since that seems to be a more recent escalation."

"Okay. Sounds good. When?" The detective's eyebrows arched.

"A day or two, maybe a bit more." Pauletti sighed. "They're sifting through the entire eastern half of the country. That's a lot of crimes."

"Yeah, and probably too many unsolved. Well, we gotta—" He leaned back, eyes now on Detective Harris barging in without the customary knock on the door. "What's up, Jack?"

"Olvida's been working with tech on the CCTV cameras, looking for that jacked Jag, Boss, and we think we got a hit."

"Where?" Warner lurched to his feet.

"Cutler Ridge, west of SW 127th." Harris glanced at his Android. "Some mostly abandoned warehouses. It just came up on my Wayz."

"Okay, let's go." He grabbed his pistol and shield. "SWAT teed up?"

"Olvida says they're coming, but might be a while. One unit's in the middle of a dustup—a bank heist, I think—in North Miami, and the other is coming from something going on in Hialeah." He scrolled though his tablet as everyone exited Warner's office. "Looks like we're gonna be at least an hour ahead of any help."

"How 'bout Beck and Salinas?"

"Beck's coming. Salinas is working a case in Little Havana."

"Shit! That's kinda thin. I hate usin' patrol cops for somethin' dangerous, but—" He paused at a tug on his sleeve by Agent Yeager.

"We can fill in, Detective. Lon, Agent Swift and me. Out-of-state trafficking in stolen cars makes it Federal."

"Yeah, good. What about Agents Ashkin and Whitehead?"

"At the Miami Field Office, working on our serial killer."

"Okay. Seven of us should do it." He squeezed her shoulder. "Never know when we might need your sharp eyes and big gun too, Ina." Hurrying toward the exit, he glanced back. "Everyone mount up, and let's get movin'. Maybe SWAT'll show in time ta help."

The FBI agents strode toward their team in the conference room, and three minutes later all were on the move. Harris with Warner in his Charger, Bech with Olvida in his Chevy, and the three BAU agents in their usual black Chevy Suburban SUV.

Warner shaded his eyes against the glare of the westerly sun and peeked around the edge of the metal storage building, then back at the six officers in his team. "No movement out front." He eyed Olvida. "The warrant come through, Ralph?"

"Yeah, Boss. Just now. Unlimited scope." He handed his Android to Warner who scanned the page before giving it back.

"Okay, so, we're legal. Anyone got an ETA on SWAT?" A forearm brushed his sweaty brow.

"Looks like nothing soon, Boss," Harris said. "The North Miami bank heist is still unresolved, and the Hialeah team's been hung up on their case, too." He glanced at his tablet. "Gonna be at least an hour, probably more."

Warner looked at his watch and shrugged. "I hate lollygaggin', but we'll try to wait it out as long as the scene stays quiet, but if they start movin'—" He jerked up at the rumble of an overhead door rising. He edged around the corner of the building and spied two men, carrying what looked like AK47's, step from the warehouse. Their eyes swept in both directions before turning back and waving.

"Well, that solves *that*. No more waitin'. Let's go, guys. Weapons hot, and don't take any chances. I ain't losin' any of my team today." He charged out, a Mossberg 12-gauge pump, loaded with 00 shot, at the ready. Harris and Olvida trailed close behind, both armed with M-4's, followed by Agents Pauletti and Swift. Agent Ina Yeager was sprawled behind her Barret sniper rifle in the open, rear doors of their Chevy Suburban, parked a hundred feet up the street with a clear field of view of their target.

"Miami Police!" Warner shouted. "Don't do anything stupid—"

One of the perps spun around squeezed off a wild burst of automatic fire, bullets pinging off the building's side and ricochetting off concrete pavement. Steel hornets whizzed past Warner's ear, but before he or his team could react, the gunman went airborne backwards, his weapon continuing to chatter harmlessly into the sky, and skidded down onto his back, blood gushing everywhere. Agent Yeager had put a

.50 slug into his chest quicker than Warner could blink. The second guy bolted for the door, firing ineffectively, and his quick move saved him from Yeager's second round that harmlessly tugged his sleeve as it zipped by.

The six cops hurried to the open door, weapons ready, but paused as Warner raised a fist. He dropped to one knee and peeked around the frame, eyes sweeping the room. The scent of fresh paint wafted out. Several fancy cars, most in various states of refinishing, and four thugs, all crouched behind benches and vehicles. And a one-car overhead rear door. He signaled to one of the patrol officers wearing sergeant stripes.

"You and one of your guys grab a car and pull around back." He nodded toward the opening. "There's a rear overhead back there they might try ta slip outta. Pull close ta block it and get ready, in case they give it a try."

The man nodded and scurried off, grabbing the arm of one of his men as he went. A moment later, Warner heard the vehicle pull away. A glance back, and he saw Agent Yeager, lugging her Barret .50, entering an empty building across the drive. Probably seeking a sniper's perch to offer his team more overwatch, as she'd done several past times.

Warner edged close to the opening and yelled a repeated message. "Miami Police. Ya got nowhere ta go. No reason ta die here."

A blast of automatic gunfire clanged off the door frame, but there was no other reply. Agent Swift went prone and wiggled forward to glance into the room.

"Looks like they're trying to work their way to a big SUV, Detective," Swift said. "Gonna make a run for it, I'm guessing."

"Miller." Warner spoke into his radio. "You got that back door blocked yet?"

"Just pulling into position, sir."

Warner heard the rumble of the squad car's engine die.

"We're teed up now. They're not gonna get by us this way," came over the radio.

"Okay, but stay alert, in case they try ta ram you. They got a big GMC SUV they're tryin' ta get to."

"Copy that. We'll be ready."

Warner glanced at the building across the drive. "Hey, guardian angel, ya in place yet?'

"Top floor window, Detective. Covering your butt again." A soft chuckle.

"Always happy ta have you doin' that, kiddo." He gestured toward the open door. "Can ya put a round or two inta the engine block of the SUV?"

"My pleasure." A moment later, two .50 cal slugs, five seconds apart, exploded into the GMC's engine. "A shame to mess up that nice truck,' came over the radio, "but they're not going anywhere in that today."

Warner nodded and again eased close to the doorway. "Ya got no way ta get away," he yelled. "Give it up now. We don't wanna kill ya."

This elicited another barrage of gunfire, and Warner saw some peppering Agent Yeager's window.

"Ina! You okay?"

"Yeah, but those crumbs just stirred up my hornet's nest."

"Good. We're goin' in now, so give us some cover." He signaled his team to get ready and rechecked the load of his 12 gauge.

"Here we go," over the radio, elicited a steady stream of six big slugs, peppering the inside. An audible grunt indicated one of the thugs hadn't found adequate cover.

Warner signaled to go, and the four of them skittered

across the doorway, weapons laying down a suppressing fire. Warner dropped to one knee and spied a perp behind a heavy bench, brandishing a machine pistol. Warner peppered both his exposed legs with a 00 blast from his shotgun, and he toppled to the ground, screaming. Odors from gunfire and the coppery scent of blood permeated the air. Then the squeal of the rear door cycling up was followed by a curse from within.

"¡Mierda! Bloqueado."

An olive-skinned guy darted from behind the SUV, weapon at full discharge, and three bullets from Olvida's M-4 slammed into his torso simultaneously with a .50 from Yeager's Berret taking off the top of his head.

"No mas, no mas," rang out from behind the cars, and after a few seconds, two assault rifles and a pair of handguns skittered across the concrete floor. The remaining perps edged into view, their hands clasped behind their heads.

Warner yelled, "On yer knees."

The two BAU agents hurried up and applied cuffs. Olvida struggled up from a crouch and limped toward the thug Warner took out with his shotgun. He grabbed some electrical wire off a bench and fashioned tourniquets high on both his thighs. Warner's blast had damaged the femoral arteries on each leg, and he'd soon bleed out if they weren't staunched.

"You okay, Ralph?" Warner grasped his detective's shoulder. "You hit anywhere?"

"Nah, Boss. Just banged my knee when I dropped to the floor." He chuckled. "Lots of bees buzzed over my head, though." He looked at the fallen crook. "Better call a bus for this guy. He was nearly a goner." Cell phone in hand, he dialed 911.

Warner massaged his eyes, then they swept the room.

The takedown lasted less than a minute. The cuffed crooks were herded into a corner, guarded by Harris and Agent Swift.

Warner turned back to Olvida. “Note which handgun belongs to which perp, Ralph. I suspect ballistics can pinpoint the murder weapon of the Jag’s owner. We got a litany of crimes here,” casting his eyes over five luxury cars, including a Porche 911 and a classic Rolls Silver Shadow, “but I’m guessin’ only one perp is goin’ down for Murder One, if he’s still even alive.”

“On it, Boss.” He gestured at the Jaguar E-Type coupe, now sporting a shiny, racing blue paint job. “Looks like they were getting ready to ship some of these out.”

“Yeah. We gotta get forensics in here, and cyber guys ta follow the bread crumbs. Where were they goin’, who’s handlin’ the shippin’, the money angle.” He watched Agent Pauletti approach. “This is Federal stuff, Lon. Probably should be your people following this up. I’m guessin, lookin’ at this setup, this may be just one arm of a bigger operation. Might lead ta a big sweep.”

“I agree.” He cocked his head and turned at the sound of arriving footsteps, and spotted Agent Yeager entering, cradling her big sniper rifle. “Good shooting, Ina. Saved Warner’s ass again.” They all laughed. “That’s getting to be a regular thing.”

“Sure makes things easier, knowing you got our six, Agent.” Warner said.

Pauletti nodded and said, “I’ll get on this with Miami, and they’ll coordinate with Quantico, if needed. This is pretty much out of our bailiwick.”

“Good ta know, ’cause we still need you guys for our serial killer. Me and my team are gonna head back to HQ. When ya talk with Miami, see if they found anything on similar MO cases." He waved to his three detectives. "C'mon, guys. Back to HQ, and let's find this crazy bastard who's killin' all those lovely cougars."

Two patrol cars and a transport van had arrived at Harris's summons, and a EMT for the wounded perp, barely still alive. While they were loading up, Warner again found Agent Yeager.

"Again, glad yer around with that big Barret of yours, when I need ya."

"Looked like you guys had it taped, Detective, but I figured, why wait and see? And your idea of putting their SUV out of order cut their options. Always glad to be of service."

Grinning, Warner clapped the Amazon on her shoulder. "Always nice havin' a guardian angel, ma'am." Turning from the chuckling agent, he waved in his team.

"Let's go, guys. We still got a serial killer ta catch."

A minute later, the two cars headed northeast, back toward Miami-Dade HQ, hoping something good had turned up while they were busy being cops, doing cop stuff.

The dashboard clock showed it was late afternoon, so Warner had plenty of time to tie things up at the office and get home early.

Can't be late for this evening's shindig. Those are the people who count.

~ 19 ~

Warner savored the aroma of roasting meat as he surveyed the six-foot folding table in his den, festooned with plates of cookies and pastries from a local French shop, and centered by the mocha frosted cake, inscribed on top with, "Happy-B Day MOM". A row of nine candles skirted one side, with two larger ones perched in the middle. Trying to put ninety-two on the cake would have been a fire hazard.

He smiled at Eva, who arrived toting two pitchers of ice water toward the dining room table, covered with Eva's best, gold linen cloth. Four bottles of Israeli wine, two Shiraz and two Cabernet, sat in the middle, and ten dinner plate setups sat ready to accept their guests.

"Looks like everyone's makin' it, darlin'," Warner said, folding her in his arms, his lips brushing her graceful neck. She quivered and glanced at little Andrea who'd dozed off, snuggled in her highchair, then turned and placed a finger on his lips.

"Not now, Al. People will be arriving—" Cut off by the doorbell. "See!" Wriggling free, Eva hurried to admit their first guests of the evening, Captain Santiago, Jack Harris, and Raphael Olvida. Buff, their rescued golden retriever, met the arrivals at the door, a paw offered for a shake from familiar visitors.

Warner greeted and shook each man's hand. "No surprise Harris and Ralph are first when there's a party goin' on, Cap. But you ..." He trailed off.

"We came together, Al." They strolled into the den. "Love to be able to celebrate that sweet lady's ninety-second.

She's a firecracker." Santiago studied the dessert array. "She make these?"

"The pastries are from Le Bon Bon, and the cake's from Publix," Eva said and delivered a playful slap on the back of Harris's hand as he reached for an eclair. "Dinner first, you sneaky guy," then turned back to the captain. "Not going to be as good as if Adele made them, but we couldn't ask her to bake for her own—" Again interrupted by the bell. It was Adele's three afternoon bridge ladies. All sifted into the den where Warner was serving drinks. Settled on chairs and sofas, Buff nagged Santiago into a vigorous ear-scratching.

A few moments later, the guest of honor arrived with her sister, Kira, who'd flown in from Haifa to help celebrate. Warner greeted Adele with a hug, who then stepped to Andrea's chair for a nose tweak and kiss on the forehead. The baby giggled and patted her wrinkled cheek. "Love you, grandma," she said.

Warner told them he planned on some private time with Kira to catch up on any final details after her last visit, where she helped ID his last mass killer. Once a Mossad agent, always a Mossad agent, even at eighty, Kira was the youngest of the five Yaacov children. Only she and Adele still lived, the three middle brothers having died in Israel's continued Arab conflicts.

"Everyone's here now," Eva said, "so let's eat. Al's carved the tenderloin, and platters are set up, buffet style," gesturing toward the breakfast room counter. "There're sweet potatoes, cole slaw, veggies, and salad. Help yourselves." The scent of tenderly roasted meat teased their salivary glands.

"Smells great," Jack Harris's tongue swiped his lips, and to no one's surprise, he was first in line.

"Bottles of wine on the table," Warner added, "so help yerselves. Mom," taking Adele's elbow, "you sit here at the head of the table, and I'll serve ya. Ya like it cooked medium, right?"

She nodded and stroked his cheek, then surveyed the dessert table as she went by. "Looks nice ... for store-bought," uttering a soft chuckle.

"Won't compare ta anything you'd make," Warner held her chair, "but we wouldn't ask ya to bake fer your own party." He patted her shoulder. "The French stuff's pretty good, though."

The other guests returned with full plates and settled at the table as Warner went to make plates for Adele and himself.

Idle chatter was at a minimum as everyone dug in. Eva was a great cook, and delicious food and heady aromas required little conversation.

Warner's eyes swept the table as he chewed a tender piece of juicy beef. He was surfeit not only of food but for the sense of family ... none of them other than Andrea, related by blood. He'd never enjoyed any of that as a kid, with real kin. Northern Illinois was far away. This, his adopted clan and friends, was much better. Buff settled at his feet, his chin resting atop Warner's foot.

Forty minutes later, the meal was consumed and the table cleared of all but dessert plates and forks. Warner rose and moved behind the honoree, clinking a fork against his wine glass.

"I wanna thank ya all fer comin' to help me honor this terrific lady, whose been my adopted mom fer the past eleven years." The tinkle of wine glasses tapped by silverware echoed through the room.

"Adele Greber and I somehow came to fill voids created in our lives. Her's first by a son, lost at war, and a husband lost to cancer. And mine to fill a hole never done by my real parents ... an abusive father and a worn-out mom who had nothing left for us.

"Most of ya know that if it wasn't fer a local cop and a math teacher/football coach, I'd probably never got here alive. They put me on the right track, and Adele here ... well, she centered me and kept me there." He raised his glass."

"So, here's ta a ninety-two-year-old wonder, one of the three most important people in my life." Leaning down, he kissed her cheek, then raised his glass. "L'chaim," and took a sip, as the Hebrew salute echoed throughout the room.

"Okay," Adele's voice choked, "enough of this." She glanced back at Warner, tears trickling from her eyes. "Let's try some of that lovely dessert."

"First, we gotta sing Happy Birthday." Eva carried the cake, candles lit, and everyone sang the song. Adele blew them out with one breath, rose, and began cutting the cake. She was, after all, the expert. And pastries began to disappear from the other platter. Again near-silence filled the room as they ate, while Eva served decaf coffee. Andrea, decked out in a yellow duck-covered bib, cooed in her chair beside her mom, her large eyes watching all as she sucked on a sippy-cup of juice.

Thirty minutes later, most had retired to the den. Adele's three bridge players begged off and had already left. Captain Santiago and Warner's two cop friends huddled in a corner talking shop, and Eva sat with the guest of honor. Warner perched on an armchair, Buff curled at his feet getting an ear-scratch, as he talked with Kira.

"So, I heard from Glick about a month ago," she said. "Seems pretty fully recovered from the broken ribs and bruised heart muscle."

"Yeah." Warner rubbed the itchy scar, hidden by a mop of hair, just above his right ear. "I check in with him every so often, but it looks like it all ended with the assassin's death. Nobody else lookin' for vengeance."

“Thank God,” Kira said, and patted his hand. “Lovely thing you did for my sister, Al. And all those heart-felt things you said ...”

“No hyperbole there, Kira. Meant every word of it.”

“Of course. And you know, you’re just as important to her.” She sighed. “With me six-thousand-miles away, no one else to look out for her, and at her age ...”

“Age is a state of mind for her, and there, she’s still young ... and making wonderful pies.” They both chuckled. Warner eased back, hands folded across his belly as they talked. At least for that night, death and terror took a back seat.

Tomorrow was another matter.

~ 20 ~

Al Warner glanced at his watch as he hurried up the stairs of HQ: Eight-ten. *Shit!* He was usually at work by seven, but after most guests left Adele's party the previous evening, he'd talked with her sister, Kira, for an hour. With over thirty years as a Mossad Special Ops handler, she was a fount of information on investigations and action plans.

Afterwards, he'd made love to his glorious wife, who, in true redhead tradition, had seemed insatiable. And that took time ... a lot of time ... because they *did* make love. Not just have sex, but slow, teasing, arousing love, a bridge to her multiple orgasms. Nothing was more satisfying than giving her ultimate pleasure. So, he'd over-slept that morning, and was late.

He burst through his department's door and spied his two top detectives, Harris and Olvida, in a gaggle with the five BAU special agents. Maybe good news on their killer? He headed for Agent Pauletti who turned to greet him.

"Got an update, Lon?"

"Of a sort, Al, but nothing definitive on our Unsub. Better news on the chop-shops though." He turned toward the conference room, now used as their office, and waved Warner to follow. The eight of them entered, settled around the oval oak table, centered by the usual box of donuts and rich smelling coffee, and Pauletti picked up a file.

"Quantico is running the search for the eastern half of the country, and so far, we've got two possible hits, one in South Carolina three-years ago, and another in Virginia, five-years ago, both unsolved strangulation murders of fortyish, black-haired women, killed in similar scenarios, but neither with the knife wound to the heart."

Warner accepted the file and began scanning as Agent Pauletti continued.

"Agents have been assigned to investigate to see if they fit this MO, and they're still working the algorithm, looking for others. It's a big area, and we're digging back for fifteen years." He leaned back, sighed, and knuckled his eyes. "Frankly, Detective, I'm embarrassed that the Department never put this together as a serial killer."

"No reason ya shoulda, Lon. Local cops don't report murders to the FBI unless they think there's a federal connection." Warner handed back the file. "Unless they have more'n one with the same MO, close enough together ta remember the connection, ya wouldn't hear about 'em."

"Yes, well, unfortunately, many don't have an Al Warner, with an elephant's memory about details." He reached for another, thicker packet of papers. "However, we *do* have better news on another front." He slid the file to Warner. "Our cyber wiz team was able to dig a lot of data from that chop-shop you busted, which led us to seven more, all located in Florida, Georgia, and South Carolina." He leaned in, forearms rested on the table.

"Teamed with local PD's and their SWAT teams, all were raided"

"That was quick. They got all that in just one day?"

"Yes. Didn't want to chance the word got out about our bust, and spook them. About thirty high-end vehicles were recovered. Most were being repainted and readied for international sales, which will bring them a lot of federal prison time."

"Any problems with the busts?" Warner skimmed the files.

"Two brief gun battles with three dead perps and one wounded agent, but overall, quite successful."

"Wow!" Warner looked up from the file. "They seem all connected. A RICO case fer you guys?" Warner's eyebrows arched.

"Looks likely." Pauletti accepted the returned file. "Justice is starting to dig in, but based on early info, the shops seemed loosely connected. We're sending what we have on apparent European and South American buyers to Interpol to try to close down that end of the pipeline." Pauletti eased back, arms folded across his chest and grinned. "Not the first time Detective Al Warner has aided federal law-enforcement in busting a widespread crime ring." Leaning back in, he collected his papers.

"Anyhow, the minute we have any info on more possible connected murders of fortyish, dark-haired women, you'll be the first to know, Al. Should have the final tab by the end of the week. You are one of a kind, my friend, and always my honor to work with you."

"Back at ya, Lon. Yer team's the only Feds' I enjoy workin' with. Most wanna take over the case and box us out. Meanwhile, I'm just doin' the job best way I know how."

"Better than most, Detective. Better than most," as they all rose. "Seems like every time we work together, it's *you* who breaks the case. We're just happy to help."

"And save your ass, now and then," Agent Yeager delivered a playful punch to his bicep.

"More'n once, Ina," Warner rose and patted her shoulder. "You're like havin' my own personal guardian angel. Can I keep you?" Everyone laughed.

"In your dreams."

A round of chuckles filled the room as Warner followed the BAU team out. He was headed for his office, and the least pleasant part of his job: paperwork. Two "usual" murders to review, needing detectives assigned, and reports to write. That job had become a bit less odious when Harris showed him how to use voice to dictate the report and watch it appear on his screen as a Word document. Pretty neat.

As the report whirred quietly from the printer, his mind drifted to his serial killer. When was he going to hit again in his bailiwick, and would he leave anything this time for them to track him down? He grunted and shook his head. What had things come to when he was eager for the next victim? If she arrived in his back yard, it damned well better be his last. Warner intended to see to that, personally.

~ 21 ~

He lingered alone, hands in his pockets, eyes following the last of his group as they exited the Roanoke Residents Inn's lobby. Their ninth season ended the previous evening to a standing ovation at the local community theater, and the eighteen of them were dispersing to someplace else. Anyplace else, after a grueling, eighteen-city-hopping tour.

He sighed. Sixteen weeks now with no schedules before starting their tenth and final run, touring, as usual, the southern and the southeastern states. The perfect vehicle for him to search out and punish wicked women. How to continue achieving that after next year's final season was something yet to be determined. The touring play was the perfect medium, and the flawless disguises to hide from the so-called authorities what he was accomplishing. People who never protected the innocent, but would be quick to punish him for doing their job, were he ever caught. Unlikely, as long as he was careful not to leave any telltale evidence that the many bitches he'd punished so far were in any way connected.

Another sigh. Time to get moving, so he returned to his room for his single suitcase and then checked out, paying his bill with his VISA card. His white Chevy Equinox awaited him in the hotels lot, fully gassed and ready for the two-day drive to Miami. The plan was to spend at least two weeks there, maybe patrolling South Beach and upscale Miami watering holes, seeking more fun and games. He wasn't sure, if he did find another sinner, that he'd take the opportunity to discipline her. It was less than a month since he'd punished Serena Redding there, and chastising another so close together might trigger a connection with the cops. He'd found no one in his last two cities that required his discipline, so Miami was his last. He hoped he'd be able to control the need when he returned there, but he knew from experience that was really hard to do.

His bag stowed inside the SUV's rear hatch, he lingered behind the steering wheel, savoring memories. Kismet had drawn him into this career and this touring show that somehow mimicked his quest, offering him the ideal vehicle for finding and punishing wicked women with little likelihood of being discovered. Eighteen so far had paid for their sins, and there would be others. He knew that. And, he realized that's what drew him back to Miami, which had proven, three times, to be a hotbed of sin.

He shrugged, sighed, and fired up the engine, knowing in his heart if he found another clone of his mother, he wouldn't resist bringing her to justice. *His* justice. No judge, no jury. They'd ultimately fail him. It was his job ... his crusade ... to rid the world of these feckless women.

Once that opportunity was fulfilled, he'd decided om a move on to central Florida, maybe Orlando or Tampa, or even Sarasota, which had become an upscale haven for the rich and decadent. Their play had never toured in those cities, but St. Petersburg was on next season's schedule. Sarasota, a short drive south, was a place such a woman might live. He had sixteen weeks, and a lot of the South to roam. Again, he steeled himself not to be too eager. Too many prizes reaped might trigger a deeper investigation that could eventually lead to him. He had no fear for himself, but worried no one would pick up his crusade to punish these women if he were caught.

Exiting the lot and headed for Highway 220 which

would eventually lead to I-95, his route back to South Florida. In no rush, he might stop in Titusville and look for a guide to do a half-day fishing on the Banana River for sea trout or redfish. A pleasant, peaceful way to unwind before beginning the serious business of crime and punishment. Stalking a flat with a flyrod for these feisty fish was a pleasure he'd enjoyed as a boy ... one of the few good memories of his father.

Then off to Miami and Miami Beach, and mixing the pleasure of casual sex with meting out punishment. He had little doubt there would be many candidates, but he *must* limit it to one before moving on.

~ 22 ~

Warner tilted forward in his chair and pulled up to his desk. Twenty minutes of quiet, free-wheeling thoughts hadn't gotten him any closer to a new avenue to pursue, looking for their elusive serial killer. Still awaiting results from the FBI's scrub of data, back as far as fifteen years, looking for a pattern. Meanwhile, he had an after-action report to review and file. He just *loved* paperwork.

A shuffle of his paper-strewn desk provided what he sought: the after-action report on their takedown of the carjacking ring. Luckily, mostly due to Special Agent Ina Yeager's sharpshooting, there'd been no injury to any of his team. The perps hadn't been so lucky. One dead and two wounded but alive, hospitalized and under guard.

Eight very expensive cars had been recovered, mostly already repainted. VIN numbers not yet altered would reveal proper owners, and once no longer needed for evidence, they'd get them back, mostly undamaged except for the new paint jobs. Meanwhile, the FBI's forensic analysts had dug up a loosely connected ring of nine similar operations in the Southeast and had taken several down and were in the process of raiding others.

Warner reviewed the detailed account, written by Detective Beck, made a few notes for more facts, and set it aside. Beck would rewrite it and submit it to the chief for approval. They'd already received clearance for discharged weapons and waived needs for counseling. No one had suffered any trauma on his team.

Eyes drawn to his door at a soft rap, he waved in Special Agent Pauletti, who was toting a moderately thick file.

“Good news, Lon?” He settled back in his chair.

“I suppose, if you consider eighteen deceased, black-haired, fortyish women good news.” He perched on a side chair and set the file on Warner’s scarred oak desk.

‘Eighteen!” The detective lurched erect. “And there was never anything connectin’ them?” Both hands slapped the desk’s top, and he shook his head. “Sorry. Not bein’ critical, but that’s a *lot* of vics.”

“Agreed, but there was nothing singular, like the more recent knife wounds to the heart, to tie them together ...” He smiled at Warner, “until my favorite cop made the connection.” He slid the file in front of Warner.

The detective grunted, snatched up the folder, and began scanning its contents. “Damn, looks like he started about eight, nine years ago, taking two or three a year. Florida, Georgia, North and South Carolina. Even two in Virginia.” He continued paging through the documents. “Never two the same week in any town, right?”

“Correct, but two to four in the same city, over the years.”

“Almost like he’s got a specific travel schedule. Business—or maybe monkey business—in each locale, that he comes back for, year after year.”

“Looks that way. We’ve got tech digging into what goes on in those cities during the weeks of the murders, but there are a lot of possibilities: conferences, conventions, expos, fairs. Things like that. Lots of data to dig through, looking for commonality.”

“Yeah, but even if ya find a common venue, there could be dozens—even hundreds- of people at those things, any of which could be our perp. Gonna be a mammoth task to sift through all that. Gotta see who’s there each time he killed.”

"Right, but that's what we do, Al. First, we've got to find the common thread before we can even begin digging."

"Good luck with that, Agent," Warner's chuckle contained no humor. "Lucky you guys got the tools for it, but I'm guessin' we ain't gonna have anything interestin' for a while, huh?"

"Could be weeks, Detective. Unless we get lucky. But even if we find a possible connection, we'll still run the complete analysis of all the attendees, in case there're more than one."

"I get it." Warner rubbed the crease beside his nose. "Ya know, I'll get my guys ta go back over the dates of our three killin's and see if we can find some commonality with those. I got some pretty good tech whiz's here too." He rose and moved around his desk as Pauletti stood to join him.

"The more I think about it, the surer I am there's some kinda tie-in."

"Agreed," the special agent said as they exited Warner's office. "I'll give Quantico a heads up on what we're doing here, and we'll keep plugging."

"Good. Just hope something pops before another body drops somewhere."

"Me too, Detective." He patted Warner's shoulder. "I suspect, knowing you, you've got mixed feelings about whether that occurs in your venue or not. I know you really want to take this guy down yourself."

"Yeah." Warner paused, turned, and shook the agent's hand. "If there's gonna be another vic, I sure want the shot at finishin' this. You get your team on scrubbin' fer commonalities, and we'll do the same here."

Pauletti nodded. "It's only a matter of time. Sooner or later, he's going to make a mistake.

Warner grunted. "Sooner the better." They bumped knuckles. "I hate these bastards more'n anything."

They strode off, each mulling what needed to be done to end the killings. Eighteen dark-haired, fortyish white women, dead for someone's twisted needs.

It had to stop, and he was the guy who was going to do that.

~ 23 ~

Warner trudged up the stairs toward his offices, bushed from a busy day on the streets. A mini-drug war broke out in Little Havana, with three gangs fighting over turf. Two Cubans, a Mexican, and three Colombians dead in four separate but nearly simultaneous shootouts. Teamed with Detectives Olvida and Salinas, and supplemented by Narco Detective Hector Carrera and two of his squad, they'd spent the morning and early afternoon chasing down soldados of all three gangs. Apparently, an over-eager member of the Colombians started an "unsanctioned" takeover of Cuban territory that somehow spilled into an upstart Mexican gang.

With surprising aide from bosses of each faction, four arrests were made of shooters. Ever since the big drug war between Cubans and Colombians, four years past, that virtually wiped out both gangs, Metro-Dade law enforcement had managed to keep a pretty tight lid on violence. None wanted either Warner's teams, or Carrera's, poking too deeply into their activities, and the cops, by necessity, mostly tolerated their business as long as they kept it "civil."

Warner's satisfaction at tying things up so fast was soon dampened by news of a deadly stoning in Opa-Locka. He'd groaned, and with his two detectives following, and Jack Harris en route, headed north. Bad enough to have to deal with Latino gangs. Now he had Muslim activists to handle. Luckily, most of that community was liberal enough not to harbor religious extremists who wanted rigid Islamic rule over women. But this was America, not Iran, and religious freedom could only be carried so far before running afoul of the law.

So, it didn't take long to find the perp and make an arrest, despite claims of religious persecution. There were enough local CCTV cameras in shops of the area to clearly identify the perp and three associates who'd stoned a woman to death in a local park because of an alleged extra-marital affair. Violence none of the cops had witnessed in a very long time.

Already late afternoon, Warner entered his office bullpen, and as he headed for his office, was intercepted by Special Agent Pauletti.

"Anything new on our killer, Lon?" He continued toward his door, with Pauletti at his side.

"Nothing useful. No new victim since yours. At least none that we know of." He followed Warner into his office and perched on a side chair. "It's been nearly three weeks, but his history hasn't suggested any specific time schedule." He leaned forward as Warner sat. "Some victims have been as close as two weeks, and sometimes it's been over a month."

"Could be based on his travel schedule, or maybe just not findin' a babe that met his requirements, whatever they are."

"Right. So, I've discussed it with the team, and we think it's time to deliver a profile of what we do know, and what we've surmised. I thought you should schedule it, as we've done in the past, and invite law enforcement from Broward, and maybe even Palm Beach Counties." He shrugged. "No victims in those climes ... yet, but they may still get involved, as Palm Beach did with your Prom Dress Killer."

"Yeah, okay. When d'ya wanna do it?"

"We thought Friday to give you time to get everyone organized.

"Works fer me, Agent." Warner rose and strode to his doorway. "Harris!"

"Coming, Boss." The bantam detective popped out of his cubicle and shuffled toward Warner.

"Tired, Jack?" Warner gently squeezed his shoulder.

"Been a long, busy day, Boss." He sighed. "What d'ya need."

Warner laid out the schedule for the BAU to deliver a profile on their newest serial killer, and then everyone went their own way.

Back at his desk, Warner checked his calendar. While in Little Havana, he'd discussed setting up this year's weekend boot camp for troubled teens, something he, Detective Carrera, and three other local detectives did on their own, each of the past five years. It was a rigorous and tiring operation, but with the help of two Juvie judges supplying a list of potential "campers," they'd run twenty to thirty kids through the ringer each session, camped far out in the Everglades, and usually managed to turn around the lives of six to ten each time. Gave them a purpose in life and mentors to rely on, a reason to shun gang life and look for more. A cop and a teacher did it for him, twenty-five-years ago, as a teen in Antioch, Illinois, and he was "paying it forward."

His reward was nineteen kids who'd never expected to live past twenty on the streets, had gone to college, six graduating so far, with various business or technical degrees. Made the effort worthwhile, and it was time to do it again, that year.

Warner picked up the phone, tasked to call Detectives Franklin and Ellison. Carrera would contact Jorge Ignacio, in Hialeah. Each knew their assignments to prep for the four weekends, and they'd set a date, four weeks hence.

So far, pressing crime had never prevented them from completing a session. Warner hoped this time would be no different.

Warner stood on the small, temporary stage in the large squad room and surveyed the growing crowd of mostly detectives, settling restlessly on their folding chairs. He glanced back at the three BAU agents behind him, then returned his attention to the group.

"Okay, guys. If ya'll settled down, we'll get goin' and have ya outta here ASAP." His eyes swept the gathering. "Most of ya may not know that it appears we got another serial killer operatin' on an infrequent schedule in South Florida, killin' attractive, fortyish, black-haired women. He's apparently been busy for about nine years, throughout the Southeast ..." eliciting a rumble from the crowd, "with three vics in Miami over the past four years, and eighteen we know of, overall. Apparently, a travelin' killer, with an agenda only he really understands. Ya all know this BAU team from the FBI," waving back at the three agents, "and they're gonna give ya their best shot at a profile from what we do know, in case any of it rings a bell with ya, now or in the future." He pivoted and nodded at the FBI team. "Special Agent Pauletti." Then he stepped back.

"Thank you, Detective," Pauletti said, edging forward, eyeing the group. "Unfortunately, there's still a lot we *don't* know, but here's what we do have, so far." He paused, awaiting everyone to settle down.

"We're looking for a white male, about six-feet, in his late thirties to early fifties. He apparently travels on some sort of schedule, because his victims are scattered across the entire Southeast, with victims occurring years apart in many cities. Unfortunately, we are unsure of hair color, as he's worn different wigs and facial disguises, seen in the security footage we've been able to find, but he appears to be physically fit."

Agent Ansel Whitehead, looking more like an NFL linebacker than a psychologist, stepped forward. “He’s apparently charming, but appears to be suffering from psychosis probably stemming from some sort of abuse as a child. Abuse for which he blames an attractive, black-haired, white woman, probably his mother or sister. That was undoubtedly sexual abuse, and he thinks of her as having a wicked or evil heart.”

Diminutive Cuban-American Agent Anita Solto, added, “We surmise the latter because the Unsub has begun piercing the hearts of his victims with a knife, always postmortem.” A statement that brought a rustle to the room. “That after first seducing them into consensual sex.”

“So far,” Agent Pauletti continued, “most of his victims have been recruited from meetings at lounges where singles often intermix. Two have come from web sites catering to sexual domination, which adds to our assessment that the unsub was abused as a youth, again, probably by an adult woman.” He paused and scanned the room.

“So, I realize there’s not much here for you to work with, but you should know what we’re dealing with and be alert. To date, we have very little hard evidence that may help solve these crimes. Not even good DNA evidence yet, but we *will* get that, eventually. Unfortunately, serial killers are often our most elusive unsubs, and many are never caught, so we need your antenna on full alert.” He glanced at Warner. “Detective Warner is running this show, since all three South Florida victims have been in his purview. Anything, no matter how minor it seems, should be run past him. You all know, no one is better at catching these guys than Al Warner.”

Assents rumbled through the room as the small crowd rose and began filing out.

Warner patted Pauletti on the shoulder, and the four of

them dispersed to continue their investigations, each wondering if-and-when another victim would drop.

~ 24 ~

He wended his way through the milling crowd, a Marlin's ball cap covering his shoulder length, golden hair, and savored the aromas of grilled hot dogs and frying funnel cakes. Clad in navy cargo shorts and a pale blue polo, Jason was dressed to kill—literally. Two-inch lifts in his shoes, bushy blond eyebrows, spray-on tan, with his eyes secreted behind aviator sun glasses, he was ready should he find her there.

The North Miami weekend street market seemed like a likely place to meet a woman—*that* woman—needing to be punished for her wickedness. As a bonus, he'd found a Hank Aaron autographed baseball for his sports memorabilia collection. He paused and dabbed at his sweating brow, careful not to disturb his "tan." Not yet summer, but already pushing ninety. He sauntered into the shade of a large, black-olive tree and scanned the sea of humanity, seeking out bargains, or maybe just a casual stroll. In any case, it was venues just like this where, in past years, he'd found two women in need of his attention, so he was hopeful.

The iced tea he'd purchased finished, he discarded the foam cup in a trash bin, glanced up the aisle, and began to stroll. There was a table, tended by a flouncy blonde with a nose ring and tattoos, hawking home-made, enameled costume jewelry, followed by another, offering retro dresses. Hands in his pockets, he ambled by, eyes on a constant prowl. Ahead he spied a booth sporting well-done watercolors of South Florida scenes: mostly beaches and what looked like Everglades, and several portraits. The artist was preparing to craft a likeness of a woman, perched in front on a folding chair.

"Why don't you remove that sunhat," Jason heard the man say, as he strolled closer, "so I can get a better view of your lovely face. We can add the hat later, if you wish."

Jason paused, still fifteen feet away, as she plucked off the straw hat, displaying a silky fall of shoulder-length black hair. He crabbed right for a better look and sucked in a sharp breath.

It was her! A casual smile ticked at her lips, her cobalt eyes glistening. Sporting an ivory, sleeveless blouse and a beige, knee-length skirt, she was the epitome of the woman he sought. He edged closer, hands on his hips, and flashed a saucy smile.

"Do your best work here, buddy. Rarely will you have a more beautiful subject to work with."

"Why, thank you, kind sir." Her grin widened, her dark eyes surveying him. "Sweet of you to say."

"I agree," the artist said. "My favorite subjects are mature women, unafraid to show their beauty." He set an 18 x 24 white hardboard on his easel and began a charcoal sketch.

"Do you mind if I watch an artiste at work?" Jason asked, aimed more at the woman than the man.

"Not at all," he said. "Maybe one of you, next?"

She merely smiled and winked as Jason declined the offer.

Forty minutes later, Courtney Baines paid for the watercolor rendering that did an excellent job of catching her warm beauty, and accepted Jason's offer to buy her lunch, which in this case was an open-grilled bratwurst in a bun, slathered with mustard and pickle relish, and an iced tea. They strolled the aisles together and traded easy banter.

Jason bought her a colorful, tie-dyed scarf, and she insisted on paying for a racy, black driving cap she said made him look rakish.

They seemed comfortable with each other as the afternoon wore on, and then Courtney pulled him to a halt.

"I'm so sorry, but I've got to run. There's a four-p.m. condo association meeting I must attend." She took his hand in hers. "I've really enjoyed this afternoon with you, Jason, but I'm on the Aventura board and can't miss this."

"Of course, but this doesn't have to be good-bye." He squeezed her fingers. "How about dinner tonight?" They continued to hold hands. "I've heard the Embers Restaurant, down in Miami Beach, has the best roast duckling. Can I pick you up at, say, seven?"

A short pause as she held his eyes, then, "Yes. I'd love that. And you're right. That's a super place." A quick glance at her watch. "But I *must* run now." She plucked a small note pad from her purse and scrawled out her address and phone number. "Call me about six-thirty to confirm, and I'll meet you down in front when you arrive."

"Super." He leaned in to kiss her cheek, but a quick turn of her head produced lips instead. The kiss was soft and momentary, but offered promise of more to come. His heart tumbled in anticipation as he walked her to the off-street lot where her Acura coupe was parked, and watched her drive off.

"So sweet and lovely," he muttered, "but I know the evil hidden in that black heart. You think you can hurt me again, you wicked bitch? I'll play your game, but in the end, it'll be you who pays the price. Not me. Never again!"

He found his Chevy, slipped inside, and after a quiet moment, drove back to his motel. Nearly three hours to kill before tonight's main event. Presuming that went as planned, would he remain in South Florida afterward, or move upstate somewhere? Maybe just stay and enjoy the pleasures of the fabled South Beach—if he can avoid punishing another woman after tonight. Not more than one at any stop. A cardinal rule.

~~~

He slouched on a leather easy chair, eyes drifting over Corutney's glorious nude body, spread across the rumpled, silk sheets of her king-size bed. With a soft grunt, he leaned forward, forearms resting across his bare thighs. She'd been the ultimate tease and one hell of a passionate fuck. Something, much to her clear surprise, she'd never do again.

The onyx-haired bitch thought she could dominate him again, just as she ... any many others ... had tried, but he was no longer theirs to abuse. Sighing softly, he rose and walked to the en suite bathroom where the very full condom was stripped and dropped into the toilet. He'd never been so completely drained as he was that evening. A quick flush sent it, and any DNA it may have provided, down the tubes. Several sheets of toilet paper were stripped off to wipe away any sperm remnants from his now flaccid organ, and that also was flushed away.

Back in the bedroom, redonning his thin leather driving gloves retrieved from his pocket, he strode, still nude to the kitchen and found a wooden rack filled with knives. He selected the narrow blade fillet knife, the perfect tool to still forever that evil heart. Returning to the bed, he hovered above her, sprawled form, legs apart, arms flung wide, cobalt eyes flared and filled with shock. After careful placement of the blade's sharp tip, it was plunged into an already still heart, releasing its evil forever.

As he dressed, Jason reviewed the evening, savoring everything that led to this final act of vengeance. As planned,
~~~

he arrived at her Aventura apartment a bit after seven and found Courtney, clad in a cocoa, silk skirt and beige, sleeveless blouse, waiting just inside the glass entry doors. He'd held the car's door for her, and once seated, drew the seatbelt across her breasts, leaning in to fasten it, which drew a breathy kiss to his ear.

"Such a gentleman," she whispered.

He chuckled and caressed her cheek. Then, seated behind the wheel, he drove off, her hand resting lightly, and very suggestively, on his thigh. They cruised down Collins Avenue and arrived at the Embers Restaurant thirty minutes later. As promised, the roasted duckling a l'Orange was crisp-skinned and delicious, the service impeccable, and key lime pie the perfect compliment. Two martinis each led to a relaxed evening, spiking further expectations.

After the sumptuous dinner, she'd suggested a nearby lounge where more martinis were consumed and they danced, mostly to love songs, and one tango, where Courtney displayed sensual skill. Returning to her building, he parked his Mazda, rented for this evening, in a guest spot, and one arm circled her waist as they made their way inside while nuzzling her face, eyes lowered, avoiding a clear image from CCTV cameras. Passionate kissing in the elevator also hid his face, and driving gloves were maintained right up until they shed their duds at the bedside. She became an aggressive and controlling lover, directing his use of hands and tongue, providing her two shuddering orgasms before finally submitting to actual intercourse. It couldn't have been more *perfect*.

A smile ticked across his lips at the memory as he moved around the apartment, wiping down anything that may have been touched by his bare hands. Alcohol retrieved from under her sink was used to cleanse her body, with special attention to every place his tongue may have ventured while igniting her libido.

Satisfied, Jason closed her door behind him and pulled the driving cap she'd purchased for him low over his eyes. Once he drove off, he'd find a secluded spot to replace the rental Mazda's stolen license plate with its original one, the South Carolina tag he'd used returned to his valise in the back seat. He'd dispose of that somewhere later, probably in a handy dumpster. He never used his own car when on these ventures of retribution. The wig, cap, prostatic nose, and false eyebrows he'd worn would be burned in his hotel's outdoor, open pit grill.

Nothing to tie him to the woman's well-earned discipline. Then what? He'd been in Miami less than a week and wasn't ready to move on. Maybe drop in to South Beach for a week or two, just to relax. Some of the play's crew were staying in a hotel on the beach there. Enjoy some casual sex with one of the hot babes usually frequenting those sands. Hopefully, not finding another woman needing punishment. He reaffirmed to never take more than one evil bitch in any city during a single visit. He knew the authorities would *not* appreciate his crusade as justified, no matter how wicked the women were, so he'd remained careful and in control.

Always in control.

No matter how difficult that sometimes was.

Fifteen more weeks to kill before the new season. A lot of time to avoid becoming reckless. He could do it, though, as he'd done for nearly ten years.

Be disciplined was his mantra.

~ 25 ~

Warner was snatched from his thoughts by Jack Harris bursting into his office, neglecting the usual knock first. Warner dropped his feet from his desk, shoved aside a cold cup of coffee, and leaned forward.

"What's up, Jack?" He suspected the answer to that.

"We got another one, Boss." Harris danced from foot to foot, clearly pumped.

"Another black-haired woman? Our serial guy?" Warner rose, opened his desk drawer, and reached for his Glock and shield.

"Yessir. Complete with a knife in the heart." He glanced at his tablet. "Cleaning woman found her during her weekly visit. The Hawk's on notice, and I asked the local detective to keep everyone else outta the apartment."

"Where?" He shrugged into his jacket, the pistol in his shoulder rig.

"Aventura condos. Local cop recognized the M.O. and the North Miami Beach guys contacted us."

They'd moved into the bullpen, and Warner shouted, "Olvida. Beck. You're with us."

Both detectives popped out of their cubicles, pocketing their credentials and guns.

"Where to, Boss?" Olvida said. "I'm presuming it's our serial nut?"

"Yeah. Aventura condos. Ralph, you take Beck." Warner was already at the exit. "Harris'll come with me. Let's hope this guy finally screwed up."

Moments later, the screech of tires against summer's heat-blistered pavement and blaring sirens echoed from the Miami PD lot from Warner's Charger and Olvida's Caprice. Blue and white grill lights flashing, they sped north to 185th Street, then over to Biscayne Boulevard, en route to the huge, upscale North Miami Beach condo complex and hope for a break in the case.

The two cars swerved into the sprawling Aventura complex, towering buildings overlooking a sparkling Biscayne Bay. They raced past the marina and spied the right building, marked as usual by a gaggle of patrol cars, lights pulsing, and milling onlookers. Warner slid his Dodge to a stop, double-parking in front, and Harris and he jumped out and hurried to the door. A glance over his shoulder showed Olvida's blue Caprice screeching to a halt, just behind his Charger.

The four detectives shoved through a small gaggle of onlookers and met in front of the expansive glass front, shimmering from the reflected late morning sun. Warner's raised eyebrows at one of the two cops guarding the doorway drew a response: twelfth floor. They strode inside and found the bank of elevators, entered, and Harris punched the appropriate button. They rode up in silence, each lost in their own thoughts about what they may—or may not—find at the scene.

They exited on twelve, and Warner in the lead, hurried toward the obvious crime scene, to their right, down near the end. Two uniformed cops stood at the door, and they waved the four detectives inside. Yellow crime-scene tape had yet to be deployed, but it was awash with uniformed and plainclothes police. Way too many for a virgin scene.

"Who's in charge?" Warner asked a uniformed guy.

He nodded into the room toward a tall, sparse, sandy-haired guy in animated conversation with two other probable detectives. “Detective sergeant Gerber,” he said. “More or less, anyway,” muttered as he turned back to the door.

Yeah. Less than more, it seems. Warner steeped to the man’s side.

“Detective Gerber?” Warner touched his arm and drew his glance.

“Yeah?” His face went blank. “Oh, Warner, huh?” His eyes swept over the four men. “Brought your whole crew, it seems,” and he held out a clearly reluctant hand.

“Well, yer boss called my captain and requested us ta join yer investigation.” He scanned the room. “This is the apparent fourth vic for this guy in South Florida, and I got the first three on my turf. We got the BAU with us in Miami, and if ya’d like, I can send fer our tech whiz and his team.” Head on a swivel, Warner continued to scan the room. “He’s most up on whatever little we’ve collected on this loonie.”

Gerber sighed, hands thrust into his pockets. “Might as well. We rarely see anything like this up here.”

“Okay.” He turned to Harris. “Get the Hawk and his team up here, Jack. ASAP.” He swiveled back to Gerber.

“Make a suggestion before we see the vic?”

“Sure.”

“Clear the room of all personnel except for one or two of your top investigators.” He waved at the room. “All this traffic is muddyin’ up the scene. If ya got CSU here, why don’t ya put ’em on standby until my team gets here. The Hawk is in a league of his own. Even the Feds rely on him, so you should too.”

“Okay. Makes sense, if we’re gonna be working together.” He drew over one of his men, and after a short discussion, the room began to empty. Soon there was only

Warner and his three detectives, Gerber, two of his guys, and three people, two men and a woman, sporting CSU vests.

Warner nodded. "Good move. Now, can I see the vic." He followed Gerber toward what appeared to be the master bedroom in that fancy, three-bedroom apartment. "No one's gonna touch nothing until the Hawk gets here, but we'll see what we can see 'til then."

"The Hawk, huh?" Gerber chuckled.

"Yeah. Myron 'Moe,' Gold. Two camps about the moniker. One votes fer his very large, hooked, snout, and the other 'cause his sharp eyes seldom miss much."

"And your vote?" as they entered the bedroom.

"Either. Both work." They paused at the side of the bed, the black-haired beauty sprawled naked, her hands posed to cover her shaved pubis, the handle of what looked like a filet knife protruding almost bloodlessly from her chest. Warner shook his head.

"That's our guy, all right."

"Spooky," Gerber grumbled. "Give me the chills, doing her like that."

Warner nodded. "The knife's postmortem, so not much blood." He leaned in for a closer look. "My psychiatrist wife posits he's got it in for a woman that looks like this, maybe with what he thinks is an evil heart." He straightened. "A real psycho."

"Let's walk the apartment. See if we can spot anything before the Hawk gets here." He circled the bed and studied the floor, a thick cream-colored carpet, the same as covered the floors throughout the unit. Nothing more obvious than a bare impression at the bed's side, probably from the vic and/or the perp standing there. Possible DNA, so he was careful not to infringe on the spot. Moe Gold would vacuum and swab everything,

Warner followed Gerber into the living room, where

Harris and the rest of his team were already searching.

Detective Beck joined them. “Just cruised the kitchen, Boss. The knife rack’s missing a filet knife.”

“That’s probably what’s sticking outta her chest, Dean.” He turned to Gerber. “Ya got any info on the vic, Detective?”

He withdrew his Apple tablet. “Ms. Courtney Baines. Forty-one, single, a senior market analyst for Merril. No steady beau. Makes big bucks, but so far, nothing seems missing here.” He looked at Warner.

“Not a surprise. This guy’s after retribution or vengeance, not stealin’ or scammin’. The BAU has profiled him as intelligent and middle-class. Maybe a professional of some sort.” He grunted. “He’s on some sorta crusade, and money ain’t an objective.”

They continued to stroll the floor, Harris at his side, taking notes on anything his boss noticed, which wasn’t much. They paused at the threshold of the en suite bathroom. “No one go in here until CSU arrives. If the perp left any DNA, it’s the second most likely spot.

Noises at the entrance drew them back into the living room where the found the arriving Moe Gold and his CSU team.

~ 26 ~

The diminutive CSU chief and three of his staff entered the apartment lugging their copious gear. Warner moved to greet them.

"Hey, Moe." Hands were shaken. "Ya made good time."

"Midday traffic was light, Detective." He set down his oversized metal supply case and stretched. "Same victim MO, Al?"

"Yeah. Pretty much a clone of the other three, includin' the knife in the heart." A hand on the shoulder, he turned from the Hawk to meet an approaching man. "This is Detective Sergeant Gerber, local Police. He's runnin' point, and we're here to assist."

"Thanks for the deference, Warner," said as Gerber shook the Hawk's hand, "but I'm gonna defer that position to you, if you don't mind." He sighed. "I know it's my back yard, but you've got the chops for this, way more'n me, so I'm glad to follow your lead."

"Okay, but we'll be a team here. Don't wanna step on any toes." He nodded toward the bedroom. "The vic's back here, Moe. No one's touched anything, and we've been real careful where we walked." He led the way. "I'm especially interested in her bathroom and the kitchen. Looks like the knife mighta come from a set on the kitchen sink counter."

"Sounds good. Right on point, as usual." He pivoted back into the living room. "Let me get my team's tasks assigned, and then we'll look at your lady." He glanced back at Warner. "The M.E. on the way?"

"Yep. Just texted Olvida. Aughta be here in five or ten."

"Good. He gets testy if we move a body before he's seen it the way we found it."

"Yeah, I know, but COD here is pretty obvious."

The Hawk nodded. "No doubt, but we'll wait, anyhow. Meanwhile, I'll get my guys going. Maybe we'll get lucky this time." He grunted. "These careful bastards seldom leave us much." He disappeared back into the other room, and Warner followed, drawn again to new arrivals at the entrance. Special Agent in Charge Pauletti, along with Agents Solto and Swift stepped inside.

"Ah, my favorite Feds." He shook Pauletti's hand and nodded at the other two. "Ya heard we got vic numero four up here?"

"We did," Pauletti responded, "so, I brought my two best crime scene investigators, if you don't mind."

"Not a bit. The more eyes the better." He introduced the three to Detective Gerber, and after a quick update, they all piled back into the bedroom to view the body."

"Damn, that's a beautiful woman," Solto said. "Was, anyhow."

"A real shame," Agent Swift muttered. "Anyone move the body?" He leaned over for a better view of the black-handled knife. "Not much blood. Clearly postmortem."

"Just like the other three," Warner said. "And no, no one's touched nothin'. Waitin' for the M.E. before we move her."

"Strange he posed her hands like that, covering her pubis," Solto said. "Ever do that before?"

"Not here." Warner turned to Agent Pauletti. "Any mention of that in the other cases ya found, Lon?"

Pauletti shook his head. "Not that I remember. It's a new wrinkle."

Swift nodded. "Almost like showing remorse." He

massaged the back of his neck. "Like he realizes these are *not* the woman he's punishing."

"Yes, he may be experiencing conflict between his need to act, and guilt over the results. Hopefully that angst made him less careful this time," Pauletti said.

They all turned at the arrival of someone new. The M.E. was there.

"Hi, Doc," Warner said. "We need ya to do yer prelims so we can move the body and look for evidence."

The medic nodded. "Thanks for waiting, Detective." His eyes swept the corpse. "Five minutes or so, and you can do what you wish." He withdrew a thermometer from is bag to establish a time of death, as the investigators left the room to see what else, if anything, had turned up.

Warner found the Hawk in the kitchen examining the counter, where sat a wood rack filled with a variety of knives. One slot was vacant. The tech was examining fingerprint dusting. "Clearly, where the knife came from, but wiped clean." His hand waved over the surface. "No prints anywhere."

"So, he wiped the entire counter?"

"Everything, Detective." He shrugged. "The fridge, the sink, the table, all the knobs. Very meticulous." He nodded back at the bedroom's door. "Let's see if Jackie found anything in the master bath." He started for the doorway. "And maybe Doc finished his prelims with the body, and we can start processing her and the bed."

Warner followed the little man as they moved through the apartment and into the master suite, where they spied the M.E. stowing his gear.

"The scene is yours, guys," the doctor said. "I've been called to another site, so let my team know when you're done processing the body, Moe, and they'll bag her and get her to the morgue." He trailed a hand down her cold arm. "A shame for such a lovely woman to end this way."

Warner's face drew into grim lines. "Not the first bastard we've had that turned passion into brutal death. Much to the surprise of a babe just seeking a night of pleasure."

"You're right, Al. Sorry if I sounded insensitive. I know you take these kinds of crimes personally." He hoisted his case. "Anyway, I've gotta run. I'll let you know if we discover anything unusual, once I get her into autopsy." And he was out the door as Warner turned toward the en suite bath, from where some excited murmurs were emanating. A few strides, and he pushed through the door.

"Don't tell me ya found somethin'?" He spotted the Hawk and his female assistant kneeling on the floor, securing swabs into sterile vials.

"Maybe we got lucky this time." The Hawk pushed to his feet and held up the small, glass tube.

"What is it?" Warner leaned in for a closer look.

"A few drops of semen, I believe." He bagged the vial. "The perp clearly used a condom, and he may have been a bit careless when he stripped it off to flush it." He slipped the vial into a hard plastic, snap-lock box. "We'll see when we get it back to the lab. It's a very small sample, but so far, it's all we've got." He returned to the bedroom.

"Now, we'll process the body and the bed." He surveyed the scene, hands on hips. "Don't know how he's managed not to leave at least a few hair or skin samples in the past. We'll see if he was that good again this time. Nobody's perfect, after all."

"Yeah." Warner rubbed his itching head scar above his right ear. "But serial nuts seem better'n most. Until they aren't." He grunted. "I wanna be there when he *does* fuck up." He turned and reentered the living room, just as Special Agent Solto returned, carrying a thumb drive.

"Hey, whatcha got? CCTV footage?" He joined her along

with Detective Gerber and Agent Pauletti.

"Yep. I did a preliminary review in the building's security office. Cameras in the parking lot, lobby, elevator, and corridors." She waved the drive. "Got the perp in all four places, but no clear facial shots. He knows where the cameras are."

"Anything stand out?" Pauletti asked.

"He's about six-foot, maybe a bit more, looked lean and fit, blond hair, looks like a goatee ... and he's wearing driving gloves. Probably leather, but never took them off in any of the footage."

"Okay." Pauletti nodded. "We'll get it to the lab and see if they can get anything more from it. They've been known to work miracles from what appeared to be nothing."

"Yeah, it's better'n nothin', but in the three previous deaths, he's been blond, redhead, and brunette, so he obviously uses disguises."

"No doubt," Agent Swift said, "and they must be damned good ones too, because his marks apparently never picked up on that."

"Ugg." Solto's face screwed into a scowl. "That'd sure freak me out, if I was ready to party with a guy who I found was in a disguise." She grunted. "A real red flag."

"So, he wore a disguise?" Jack Harris, who'd joined them, asked.

"Right. Anita nailed it. It should have freaked them out, and that never happened," Pauletti said.

"So, he's damned good at disguises." Warner looked at Swift. "A professional?"

"That'd be my guess."

"Something to add to the profile." Pauletti stroked his jaw. "We'll have to rework that. Maybe help narrow the field."

"I damn well hope so." Warner glanced at his watch.

"Harris, you ride back with Ralph. I gotta run." He chuckled. "Date night out with Eva, and can't be late." He paused, then touched Pauletti's arm.

"Ya say there's never *any* trace found on or around the vic? In all the previous murders?"

"Correct." Pauletti's eyebrows arched. "Why?"

"Ever check the site for somethin' like a hand vac? Somethin' like that to clean up after himself." Hands shoved into his pockets, he continued. "Seems unlikely he coulda brought one with him, so maybe he used somethin' handy there."

"Good thought, Detective." He signaled over Swift. "Bound to be full of all sorts of matter, but maybe tech can find something linked to what your guys just discovered in the john." He instructed his agent what to look for. "It'd be an arduous task, sorting through all the waste that may be there, but worth a try."

"Okay. If ya find something, ya may wanna give it to the Hawk to dig through. Free yer guys up ta broaden their search, 'specially if he gets anythin' useful from the DNA he found." He turned toward the door. "Now, I gotta run. I'll leave y'all to it."

He hurried off, his mind sifting what they'd learned, hoping what they may find. They were getting closer. A buzz from his Android phone, and he chuckled. Eva was dragging him into the 21st Century and insisted he needed a new smart phone. She'd shown him how to set up the calendar to get reminders. He plucked it from his pocket and activated the screen.

There was the notice. "Lunch tomorrow w/boot camp buddies." He gave a quiet groan, then shrugged. Time to set up a new weekend camp-out for a squad of teens facing juvenile detention. Two Juvie judges they'd work with offered Warner's boot camp to kids they thought might straighten out with proper guidance: their options were four weekends at the camp, or detention.

Warner settled in his car and sent a group text to his four "partners" in this venture, reminding them of the luncheon at Spiro's Deli, tomorrow at noon. Phone pocketed, he headed for his office, half hoping tomorrow's date would be preempted by breaking leads in their current case.

Probably unlikely to have anything so soon after the most recent death.

~ 27 ~

Warner glanced at his Dodge's dashboard display and saw it was 12:15. He was late for his luncheon meeting with his four detective buddies to discuss the start of their fifth, four-weekend boot camp for troubled juvies, and he hated to keep them waiting, but the Hawk had called him with preliminary info on their quick DNA results from the Baines crime scene. He had a DNA profile, but unfortunately, no quick match. The Hawk set up a search with the Federal systems, and that might take a while. At least when they caught the bastard, they'd have it for a match.

Warner slid his coupe into a diagonal slot in front of Spiro's Deli in Miami Springs, a more-or-less central spot for the five of them to meet. Striding through the glass entry, he inhaled the heady aroma of baking cinnamon and garlic. He spied the four men gathered around a table for six, under the glare of fluorescents, along the rear wall. Hector Carrera, a NARCO detective from Little Havana noted his approach. He smiled and waved.

"The Hero arrives," he chuckled.

Warner grunted and slid onto a chair. "Gettin' a little stale, Hector."

"Nah, Al," Ben Ellison, homicide guru from North Miami, quipped. "You'll always be our Hero, buddy."

"Yeah, yeah, some hero." He bumped shoulders with Darnell Franklin, a B & E cop from Overtown and nodded to Jorge Ignacio, Gangs and Organized Crime, from Hialeah. "Glad we all made it." He looked at Carrera. "You check the site?"

"Yeah. As usual, it's gonna need clearing out. Damned 'Glades are relentless, but other than being overgrown, she's pretty much the same." He withdrew an iPad, laid it on the table, and tapped it. "The highway department'll put up signs early in the week so no one can claim they got lost."

"Okay, Warner stroked the screen of his new Android phone. "I've talked to clerks of both judges," glancing at the screen, "and—"

"Look at that!" Ellison gestured at the phone. "Al Warner's come into the twenty-first century," eliciting a round of chuckles.

"Eva's dirty work." He grinned.

"Well, good for her," Ben Franklin said, and delivered a playful punch on Warner's shoulder.

"Yeah, I gotta admit, it ain't so bad." He activated his Notepad. "Anyhow, got twenty-eight names of juvies the judges felt there was some hope for." He eased back in the chair. "The clerks are gonna give 'em all a heads up and the ultimatum: our four weekends camp or juvie lockup. Should have the final list by next week."

"Sounds good," Ignacio said. "Sixteen, I think, are Latino." He turned to Warner. "All boys, I presume."

"Always," Warner replied, as he scanned the names. "We got enough problems with guys without mixin' in hormones." His eyes caught Franklin's. "You checked the tents, cots and tables, Darnell?"

He nodded. "Visited the storage locker this a.m. Everything's in good shape, and thanks to couple a of new donors, we got better cots this time."

"I got two delis and a restaurant committed for food," Carrera added. "Havana Café's gonna loan us a complete propane hot service tray line for the evening buffets. They'll even set it up for us, day before."

Warner nodded and plucked up a menu as their waitress

approached. "Five years of doin' this has apparently earned us a pretty solid rep, guys." Said to murmured agreement.

"It's neighborhood guys who come through, Al," Ellison said, setting aside his menu. "Getting these kids off the street is a boon to most of them."

Conversation paused at they ordered, mostly sandwiches on rye, and a few of the delicious-smelling cinnabuns.

Some details were ironed out while they awaited their food, each man with specific assignments. The kids would arrive on a Friday, all before three p.m. After a brief orientation, the first task would be cleaning out the overgrown vegetation, a good, sweaty workout to burn off some hyper energy. Then set up bed assignments in the three sleeping tents, and a half-mile run before dinner, something the teens all hated.

The intent was to tire them out and give tasks to create an order. Some would rebel, but Warner's posse had four consecutive weekends to whip them into shape, and often the most rebellious at first became their most committed to change by the end.

It was what an English teacher/football coach, and a cop, did for Warner as a teenager in northern Illinois. It worked for him, and he was committed to paying it forward. It also provided a rare social interaction for him and four guys ... colleagues ... who had become good friends, all with a common purpose. The more successful they were, the fewer kids they had to deal with on the streets. They'd developed long-term mentorships with a few of their graduates. Six from earlier sessions had already completed college and moved on to successful careers.

It was after three when they dispersed, back to their jobs catching criminals. Warner headed in for a brief stint at HQ to see if anything new had popped. Then, Eva was taking him out to dinner to an Italian restaurant they'd enjoyed two years ago.

Free time with his beautiful, redhead wife regenerated his soul, and luckily, his "mom," Adele, loved caring for Andrea when they were both away.

Warner suspected there might be warm, freshly baked peach pie awaiting their return in the evening. Even at ninety-two, Adele still loved to bake, and Warner enjoyed eating whatever she concocted. She was a whiz.

~ 28 ~

After a brief stop to check on Adele, as he did every chance he had, Warner pushed through his front door and was met by the clatter of paws on the tile entry. Buff slid to a stop and sat in front of him, offering his paw in welcome. He knelt and provided the expected ear-scratching while getting a thorough tongue face slathering. Finished, Warner rose, and the big golden followed him at heel into the townhouse. He tilted his head and sniffed, detecting no aromas of cooking food, then shrugged. They were going out to dinner, so of course, Eva prepared nothing.

"Eva?" He crossed the carpeted den floor, Buff trailing, his cold nose nudging Warner's fingers.

"In here, Al," came from their bedroom.

"Daddy's home," little Andrea called. "Kiss, kiss."

"Ahh, my two favorite women," Warner chuckled as he entered the room and found Eva, clad in a black bra and silk panties, inspecting the classic little black dress. Andre perched in the center of their bed, her toy, stuffed dragon clutched to her breast. He folded his wife into his arms for a protracted kiss and gently roaming hands.

She wiggled free. "Al! The baby." Lips tilted into a saucy grin, she caressed his stubbled cheek. "Let's get ready to go. I don't want to be late for our reservation."

"You sure?" He grinned. "We could stay home and have a *very* nice party here."

"You know I love that, hon." She stepped back and picked up the dress. "But I'm taking you out for a change.

Give that laser mind of yours a chance to relax." She slipped into the gown. "Doctor's orders, bud. Now, say 'Hi' to your daughter and then clean up and put on a nice pair of pants and one of these new shirts with the fancy cuffs I bought you." She kissed his nose, then perched at her makeup table.

Warner sighed, then settled on the bed with his now nearly three-year-old, auburn-haired daughter, gathered her into his arms, and peppered her face and neck with tiny kisses, eliciting gleeful giggles and a fierce hug.

"I love Daddy. Big and strong, and good kisses." She clasped his face between her tiny hands. "But scratchy face," followed by more giggles.

Warner tossed and twirled her, then set her on the floor. "Daddy gotta to get dressed, Andi. Mama's orders." Both laughing. "Nana Adele's gonna take care of you, and I bet you guys are gonna do some fancy bakin'."

"Yay." The girl clapped her hands. "Andi loves cooking with Nana."

"Okay." He bent and kissed the top of her silky hair. "You play with Dino while Mamma and Daddy get dressed." He headed for his closet to select the indicated outfit, then to the bathroom for a shower, shave, and to dress. The baby was where Eva could keep an eye on her ... their unexpected treasure that completed their lives.

Forty minutes later, with Andrea deposited in the safe environs of his substitute mom's connecting townhouse, they were in Eva's Jag sedan, headed south toward Coconut Grove and Bistro Italiano. It'd been two years since they'd dined there, right in the midst of the Deena Wright investigation, Warner's first inkling they were dealing with another serial killer. He remembered how great the food was, especially the side dish of linguini Bolognaise. He planned on ordering that as the main course this time.

Already past forty, Warner still had no trouble with his weight. He ran at least a mile with Buff almost every morning before heading for work, and had a small weight setup ... a bench press and barbells ... at the side of his one-and-a-half car garage. Twice he'd been thrust into comas by head trauma during the conclusions of his first two serial killer cases. He'd been rigorous at getting back into top physical condition ... and staying there. So, carbs and sweets were never a worry, or Adele would have already fattened him up with all her delectable pastries.

They arrived at the restaurant a tad before seven, and Eva relegated her Jag to the valet. The sumptuous aromas of roasting garlic and oregano brought saliva to their mouths as they followed their waiter across the dimly lit room to a small booth in the back. A string trio was warming up, adjacent to the small, polished oak dance floor.

They settled side-by-side on the plush bench, against the wall so they could look out at the room. Warner always chose to sit that way, with his back unexposed to an open room. His "Aces and Eights" complex, he called it, in deference to the cards held by Wild Bill Hickock when he was assassinated from the rear while playing poker. The waiter took their drink orders, Johnie Walker Black for him, and a vodka martini for her, and left them menus before leaving to get their beverages.

Warner wrapped Eva's shoulder with an arm, snugging her close. "This is nice, babe." He kissed her cheek. "Last time we were here you dragged me ta see that mystery play, which was more fun than I expected."

"Yes, at the Grove Playhouse." She sipped her drink, which had just arrived. "Yum." She wiggled deeper into his arms. "Actually, that same play was here again, about three weeks ago."

Warner took a swig of Scotch. "They're a tourin' company, huh?"

"I guess. I read their ad in the *Herald*. I think it's the same cast and everything."

Warner picked up his menu with the other hand, and started scanning, despite knowing what he was going to order. He paused, and his eyebrows arched. "Three weeks ago, you said?"

"Uh huh." Eva also had a menu in hand, lips pursed as she studied the offerings.

Warner hitched around a bit and caught her eyes. "That's about when our serial nut killed Redding. Three weeks ago." He rubbed his chin, then took Eva's hand. "Ya can look up stuff on that fancy iPhone of yers, can't ya?"

She nodded. "Usually," and fished her cell from her clutch. "What do you want to know?

"Can you see if that play was here another time, prior to two years ago?"

"Probably." She activated the screen, then glanced at her husband. "Why?"

"We think our killer travels on some sorta schedule, from place ta place, often revisitin' the same cities, years later."

"Like a touring play company?" She nodded, and began typing instruction to her search engine.

"Yeah. A perfect vehicle for our killer, and I bet, even plenty of makeup and disguise gear to hide his identity." His fingers drummed the table, awaiting an answer from Google, or whatever iPhones used.

A few seconds later, Eva's brow wrinkled, her green eyes raising to catch Warner's. "Four years ago, Al. Same play, same theater." She thrust the phone in front of Warner's face. "Their first trip to Miami, too."

"You got dates?" Warner signaled a passing server. "Ya got a piece of paper and a pencil I can borrow, bud?" A cocktail napkin and a pen in hand, he turned back to Eva.

She held the phone up as he copied the information. "I'm pretty damned sure that's the week Maria Santiago was killed."

"Wow!" Eva laid a hand on his arm. "So, it could be someone in the cast?"

"Yeah. Actually, anyone in their crew." He sighed.

"You're not going to ruin our evening, are you?"

He shrugged and shook his head. "Nah. I'll put in a call ta Pauletti, so he can start researching the other sites. See if the play was in those cities the week of the other murders." He kissed her cheek. "This *is* excitin', but I ain't gonna get anything done this evenin', and I know ya've been lookin' forward ta this."

He plucked his new Android cell from his pocket. "Let me make the call, then we can order dinner," his head cocked at the musical onset from the trio, "and maybe dance a few." He wrapped her in a fierce hug. "Nothin' I love more'n holdin' my gorgeous redhead in my arms, swayin' ta a sexy ballad." He punched a number on auto-dial, and chuckled to himself that he'd become so techie, thanks to his wife. It was answered on the second ring.

"Pauletti."

"Hey, Lon. Just got what I think may be our connection to our killer." He relayed what he and Eva discussed, including their recent and past visits to south Florida.

"Good catch, Detective. I'll contact the night desk at Quantico and get someone on it immediately. Enjoy the rest of your evening. It may be a day or two before they can research everything." He said his goodbyes.

Warner disconnected just as their server arrived to take their orders. He pocketed his phone, intent on not ruining Eva's night out. She worked long hours as a therapist, and needed a break as much as he did. Thay made their selections, and the waiter returned quickly with plates of luscious-smelling garlic bread and a small selection of antipasto. Warner asked him for a second round of drinks while they awaited their dinner, then rose, took Eva's hand, and twirled her onto the nearby dance floor, swaying to a classic Neil Diamond love song.

Two more ballads, then something jazzy drove them to their table, just as dinner arrived. They settled down to sup and drink, and finished it off with creamy slices of Italian cheesecake. Somehow, he managed to tamp down the electricity pulsing through him over their new revelation.

Just before ten p.m., Eva slid her Jaguar sedan into their townhouse garage, Warner's Dodge coupe sitting to one side on their drive. Not too late to retrieve a sleeping Andrea from Adele's home. She was a night-owl, and as expected, she and the infant had baked peach turnovers. Eva begged off, settling for a cup of steaming decaf, but Warner ate one of the flakey-crusted delights, despite their hearty meal. Adele's pastries were hard to resist, and peach pie was his favorite ... a fact she knew very well.

One of the few pleasant memories from his northern Illinois childhood was visiting a southern Wisconsin orchard with his high school English teacher/football coach to pick peaches. They'd raced back to Antioch and a quick swim in Channel Lake in an attempt to rid themselves of the itchy fuzz that made it inside their shirts while picking the fruit. Eating the pastry now, he smiled at the memory.

Then with Andrea cradled in his arms, they returned to their own digs and settled the child into bed. Gentle kisses by both parents didn't faze her, as none sleep more deeply than infants.

Warner and Eva returned to their master bedroom, where he pulled her into his arms for a warm kiss.

"You going to be able to sleep tonight, Al?"

"What? Oh, because of our new lead, thanks to my brilliant wife?" Still holding her close, he caressed her cheek.

"Yeah, I think so, 'cause I have some very busy plans first." His kisses more passionate now, he unzipped her dress, his fingers becoming tantalizing voyagers.

"Oh, you wicked man." She chuckled. "Planning on having your way with me, are you?"

"Damned right." His lips slid to her neck, his tongue busy.

"Good." She was panting now. "I love how you do that." She was stripping away his shirt. "I *love* you, my passionate hunk."

Soon, their clothes shed, they were on the bed, mouths and hands teasing. Never rushed, Warner spent many minutes finding all her arousal points, and they made love well into the night. Warner could never get enough of his redhead lover, nor she of him.

He once again relished this miracle, something beyond his wildest fantasies.

~ 29 ~

Warner trudged up the stairs toward his offices. It had been a busy two days, starting yesterday morning with a deadly domestic disturbance in Miami Springs that resulted in a three-hour standoff before he and Harris were able to sneak in the back door and take down the shooter without incident. He burned at the fact that the victim, a twenty-six-year-old middle-school teacher, had tried and failed to get her stalker put away before he ultimately did what he did ... kill her. A toothless restraining order did little to stop him.

On the way back to HQ, after securing the scene and sending the perp off in a lockup van, they were diverted to a liquor store heist that ended with the clerk dead and the perp on the run. A witness got the make and license number of the getaway car which sparked an APB. Racing to the scene, they spotted the culprit's Toyota speeding through a cross street and gave chase. Warner tailed the fugitive until they reached a relatively deserted stretch of road, heading toward Cutler Bay.

The perp's Carolla sedan was no match for the power and speed of Warner's Charger, and after less than a half-mile of bump and grind, the he was forced off the road and into a culvert. Shots were exchanged, and the killer took one of Warner's .40cal's in the shoulder, putting him down. Cuffed and secured in the rear of his car, they awaited an ambulance and police escort for the trip to the hospital and then lockup.

"You gonna get your car to the shop to fix those dents,

Boss?" Harris asked after the guy was carted away by an EMT emergency vehicle with a patrol cop riding security.

"Don't know, Jack." He shrugged. "This custom baby is Kevlar lined. Sorta my security blanket. Hate ta leave home without her."

"Understood, considering how many Chargers you've had shot out from under you." They'd started back toward HQ. "Motor pool aughta have something you can use, though." He canted his head as his police radio squawked.

"Detective Warner, you copy?"

He triggered the mike. "Warner here. What's up?"

"Busy day, sir. Mall parking lot shooting, possible fatality." A pause. "Detectives Olvida and Beck are on a different call."

"Patrol on the scene?" Warner asked.

"Yes sir, but they're calling for Homicide. Are you wrapped--?"

"Yeah, yeah. We were on the way in." He sighed. "Text Harris the address and we'll cover it. Where abouts?"

"Le Juene Road Mall."

"Copy. We're ten to fifteen out. Advise patrol ta secure the scene, but don't touch anything. Warner out." He glanced at Harris, who was receiving the text.

"What a fuckin' day! This keeps up, we ain't ever gonna find time to chase down our MILF killer." He flicked the emergency lights on, flashing blue and white from his grill and trunk lid, and took off for the busy north-south avenue that bordered the eastern edge of Miami International. Despite the already late hour, the early summer sun still glinted well above the horizon.

The crime scene had been easy to find with two patrol cars flashing their emergency lights, an EMT ambulance, and a gunmetal gray Infinity four door with a bullet hole in the windshield.

Apparently, Mr. Carl Wisner was returning from Home Depot and saw someone pulling his QX60 from his parking spot. Wisner raced up the drive, brandishing a Colt 9mm he was licensed to carry. The thief started to back the car away, but was blocked by a big SUV that had turned in behind him. That route stalled, he went into drive and charged forward, expecting the man to jump aside. Instead, Wisner put one very well-placed slug through the windshield and into the guy's face with deadly results.

Warner pointed out to the man that Stand Your Ground didn't apply to someone stealing your car. Wisner rebutted that the guy was trying to run him down, and his life *was* in jeopardy. That was supported by bruised thighs, a banged-up face, and his ragged appearance.

"Already had one car stolen last year," he'd muttered in response to Warner's questioning. "Never saw it again, and I damned well wasn't gonna let some creep get away with it again."

The creep proved to be an MS13 soldier with a log rap sheet of theft and assault, and while Warner was going to bring Wisner in for processing, he suspected no charges would be filed.

"Don't tell anyone I said this," he whispered to the man as he secured him in the Charger's back seat, "but as far as I'm concerned, good job. One less dangerous nut out there to hurt people."

As they headed for processing, he continued. "Gonna see if we can keep yer name outta this, so his buddies don't come lookin' for ya. Regardless, keep yer head on a swivel for a while, until this cools down. MS13 is a nasty bunch."

Warner cast aside his mental recap of yesterday's events as he reached the top of the stairs, pushed through Homicide's doorway, and headed for his office, shaking his head. Today was just as frantic, filled with two drive-by shootings, one in Overtown with two dead teens and the other in Little Havana, with a deceased woman who was out walking her dog. Both senseless and with plenty of witnesses. Residents of iffy neighborhoods were beginning to stand up against wanton violence, and they were finally catching these perps. Hopefully, community involvement would put some sort of blanket on the crime rate there.

Those two events bracketed a smash-and-grab at a downtown jewelry store. The owner pulled a gun from under the counter and shots were exchanged. The bandit was dead, and the proprietor was in critical condition. There'd been an accomplice in a car who'd raced off, but a bystander got the plate, and there was an APB out on the Ford Taurus. If the clerk died, the driver was in for accessory to murder, and when a perp brings a gun to a robbery, it's Frist Degree. The implication was, if he brought it, he intended to use it.

Warner glanced around the bullpen. Pretty empty that afternoon with Olvida, Beck, and Salinas all out on other cases, and Harris still at the Little Havana crime scene. He poked his head into the conference room and found Agents Yeager and Solto busy on laptops. They turned to greet him.

"Where's the rest of yer team, Ina?" His eyes swept the room. "Any news on whether that play's our connection?"

"Just heard from Agent Pauletti. He's on the way in with the preliminary results of the search." Agent Yeager rose and stretched, "Sounded like you hit the proverbial nail on the head, Detective." She glanced at the wall clock. "Should be here any—" They turned as the door flew open and Agent Pauletti hurried in, a thickish file in hand.

"Ah, Detective Warner. Just who I was going to see." He dropped into a chair and waved Warner into another, then plopped the file with a thump on the table. "I think we've got our link."

"The play?" Warner settled on an adjoining chair.

"Looks that way." Pauletti nodded. "*A Murder Mystery* was playing all eighteen times that each murder occurred." He opened the file. "No clue yet who might be the perpetrator, though. It's a cast and crew of fifteen men and three women. Quantico is running deep dives on every one, and that's going to take a few more days, at the least."

"So," Warner leaned in, "where are they now?"

"Unfortunately, disbanded for the summer. Their last show of their season was in Roanoke, over a week ago." He eased back and sighed. "They've all gone separate ways for the next fifteen weeks."

"They're not playing here?" Warner scratched his head. "We just had another murder. Definitely the killer's M.O."

"True." Pauletti's brow crinkled.

"Maybe some of the cast and/or crew came back here after their last show," Agent Solto pitched in. "Any way to trace their whereabouts now?"

"Already got tech working on that," Pauletti said. "If one or more are in the vicinity, that'll help narrow our suspect pool, won't it?"

"Should." Warner pushed to his feet. "But I wouldn't leave anything ta chance, Lon. The guy coulda killed and ran. Best ta profile every guy who fits the physical description in their crew. Anyone know where everyone is now?

"We hope the director, Nick D'Amato. We've got agents tracking him down."

"Good. The rest of the crew's got access to all their props and makeup too, so it ain't necessarily only an actor." Warner turned toward the door. "Could be any one of them."

"Agreed." Pauletti also rose. "We'll run profiles and histories on the appropriate men in the troupe. At least we've got something to sink our teeth into. I'll swing by, Al, once we get it all put together. If this guy's in your bailiwick, we'll need you on the takedown."

"Damned right. No way I'm gonna miss that. I hate this kinda murdering bastard more'n anything. Killing people 'cause of some twisted motive." He looked over his shoulder as he exited. "I got some reports ta finish, then I'm headin' home." He chuckled. "Been a busy two days, but you call me, Lon, the minute ya got somethin'. I don't care what the hour."

"Copy that, Detective. You'll know as quickly as I do. At least we're finally on some sort of track toward the end of this."

Warner nodded, and left the room. He settled in his office and attacked a small stack of reports, then glanced at his wall calendar.

Shit! Ten days 'til our first weekend boot camp for juvies. Hope this goddammed case don't screw that up. He sighed and went back to his paperwork, a job that never seemed finished.

~ 30 ~

The receiver of Warner's land line was wedged between his left shoulder and his ear, his ankles crossed and draped over their usual spot, the corner of his desk.

"So, Hector, sounds like you've got everything on track for next Friday." His detective friend from Little Havana had pretty much taken over as his co-captain for their DCBC (Dade County Boot Camp), especially with Warner mired in another serial killer hunt.

"Yep," Carrera replied. "Franklin's got a U-Haul and driver set up for Wednesday to deliver the tents, cots, and other stuff to the site. Ignacio and I hacked out an area to off-load it, so the kids have a start for clearing out the meadow and setting up the tents."

"When's food and supplies scheduled?"

"Three p.m., Friday. The coolers and genny should be going by then." He chuckled. "We've got it nailed, buddy. You concentrate on nabbing your serial nutcake, and we'll be ready to rumble." He paused. "You gonna make the intros, as usual? One of us can—"

"No, I'll do it. Always manage ta get away for these weekends, and this ain't gonna be any different." He glanced at the door as Agent Pauletti knocked. Dropping his feet, he waved the BAU agent in. "Gotta run now, Hector. Keep me posted."

"On it, pal," and they disconnected.

"Been two days, so I'm guessin' ya got somethin', Agent."

Pauletti nodded as he sat and laid a thickish file on the scarred oak desktop. “Preliminary backgrounds on all eighteen members of *A Murder Mystery* crew, but only six men are physically similar.” He flipped open the file. “Still digging for more, but what we’ve got is a good start.”

“Okay.” Warner leaned forward, forearms on the desk. “Clue me.”

“We’ve located the play’s director, Nick D’Amato, and two field agents are running him down. Hopefully, he’ll know where most of his people went.” His eyes caught Warner’s. “Most specifically, if any came to South Florida.”

“Any pop out,” gesturing at the file, “as our possible perp?

The agent nodded. “Preliminarily, Clive Warwick and Travis Mott.” A sheet was plucked from the file and proffered to Warner. “Warwick was the lead actor, playing the Detective, and Mott was the co-lead, playing the killer.”

“Yeah, I remember them from two years ago. Both pretty good actors, givin’ off real natural vibes.” He scanned the paper. “Ahh, Warwick’s from a broken home, huh? And Mott’s a perfect physical match, red hair and all.”

“Yes. Warwick was raised mostly by his dad. Apparently, his mom was a tramp, sleeping around, and sometimes brought guys back to their house when dad was away. Traveling salesman, usually gone for three or four days at a time.”

“Hadda be tough on the kid, seein’ that.” He handed the paper back to the agent. “What about Mott?”

“As you say, he’s a good physical match, but that’s only part of it. Quantico’s collecting his social media history, which I haven’t yet seen, but they’ve told me those from his late teens and early twenties were continual rants about how he hated his apparently overbearing and controlling mom, with implications he wished her dead.”

"That's pretty damnin', ain't it?"

"Potentially. But there're also posits from the Washington BAU psych team that Warwick's mom may have actually seduced the kid ... several times ... as a teen. Constant social media reference to her 'wicked heart,' which fits right in with the killers MO."

"Any indication why his pop stayed with her, after all that?"

Pauletti shook his head. "Didn't. Divorced her when Clive was thirteen, but according to his Facebook history, she'd come to see him when his dad was away, throughout his teens. Lots of emotional conflict in the posts, indicating he had sex with her, then hated himself."

"He wrote that?" Warner's brow wrinkled. "For everyone to read? In public?"

"Not in so many words." Pauletti shrugged. "But our psych team gleaned that from years of MySpace, Facebook, and Twitter posts. They're pretty damned good at deciphering nuances."

"Well, looks like both guys cover all the bases for our killer. Why he might fuck the women before killin' 'em, then goin' even farther to still what he perceives as an evil heart." He shoved to his feet. "Know those guy's whereabouts?"

"Not yet." Pauletti also rose and collected the file. "I'm going to get you a copy of this, and we'll go over everyone in it. Both Warwick and Mott look like our guy, but we'll dig deeper. See if we missed anything."

"Good." They started toward the office's door together. "Most obvious ain't always the right one in the end." He tugged on the Agent's sleeve. "Get me the pages on both men ASAP, though. I'm gonna have my guys see if either, or both, are in town. I hope the play's director knows the location of his people, especially if any came down here after Roanoke."

Pauletti handed Warner the two pages. "Here. Take

them now and have your guys make copies. They can get them back to me later. We get any more info on who's where, I'll get it to you, ASAP."

"Good. I'll get tech on scrubbin' all the local tourist venues, here and on the beach." He strode toward Jack Harris's desk.

"Harris." He paused in front of his chief detective's desk and dropped the pair of pages in front of the seated man, who'd been studying his desktop's screen.

"Yeah, Boss?" He looked up and slid back on his seat.

"Make copies of these and get the originals back ta Pauletti, then task tech to search Dade and Broward for these guys, Clive Warwick and Travis Mott. Hotels, credit card usage, maybe car rentals." Warner leaned a fist on the man's blue metal desk. "Start with South Beach and work out from there."

"On it, Boss." He plucked up the page. "Who are they?"

"Cast members from that murder play. They both fit our guy's profile, so they're Persons of Interest, but we're also lookin' at the entire crew."

"Got it." Harris rose and stepped to a side desk, slipped the page inside a flat, white electronic device, punched a few keys, and hit ENTER.

"Whatcha doin', Jack? That don't look like a copier."

"Scanner, Boss." He chuckled. "Twenty-first Century stuff we're just getting you into, nowadays."

"Yeah, yeah," Warner grunted. "So?"

"It scans—copies—the doc, and I sent it directly to Tech." The machine stopped its quiet hum, and Harris retrieved the paper. "Faster than me going to the Xerox machine, making a copy, then schlepping it upstairs." He plucked his phone, which had softly chirped, from his pocket, tapped the screen, the showed it to Warner.

"See. Confirmed they got it and are starting a search."

"They know that's what you wanted?"

"Yep. I typed a quick message to go with it: 'Search local, S/B 1st.' and they'll take it from there."

"I'm gonna have ta work on my tech skills, I guess. I always like paper and pencil, but gotta admit, this seems faster and more efficient." He sighed. "Eva's gonna be proud of me," and chuckled.

"So, soon as ya get somethin'—anything, Jack—you get ta me. BAU's huntin' down the play's director. See if he knows where each of his crew went, especially any ta South Florida." He folded his arms. "Now that we got DNA from the Baines crime scene, if it's one of the play's crew, we oughta be able ta ID him pretty quick."

"On it, Boss. Keep you posted." Harris settled back at his desk. "Meanwhile, I'm digging in more to that Little Havana drive-by. See if there're any gang activities there."

"Okay. Always enough ta keep us busy, huh." He gave a wave and headed back to his office, other paperwork awaiting his attention. That's the one thing that never stopped.

Paperwork.

~ 31 ~

Warner and his number two detective, Rafeal Olvida, trudged up the stairs to HQ together, bushed after a hectic romp in search of the perp from a deadly home invasion in North Miami. The call came in during their morning briefing session, and Warner went to the scene with Olvida. Harris and Detective Beck were winding up a domestic dispute murder, and Detective Salinas was in the middle of another gang shooting in Little Havana.

Often, home invasion crimes were quickly solved, thanks to the advent of doorbell cams, and this dope waited to don his ski mask right in front of the camera. A neighbor recognized the perp from the video Warner showed to everyone. He was ID'ed as a DoorDash driver who made regular deliveries to their neighborhood. The perp had noticed the woman's diamond necklace and three-carat diamond ring during a previous visit and returned to snatch them. The husband, who wasn't supposed to be home, was. He fought and died from several knife wounds.

A quick call to the local DoorDash franchise secured the guy's route that day, something he'd continued, thinking he was safe. Warner and Olvida got to his next delivery first, and with the apartment dweller in his den, they were there to answer the bell. The guy's eyes flared at the sight of the detective, and he bolted, Warner hot on his heels. That chase ended inside of a hundred yards, with a flying tackle. High school football skills not forgotten. A short struggle had the killer in cuffs.

Harris's quick search of his vehicle found the jewelry in a small cloth bag in the center console. A pat-down after he was cuffed produced a four-inch, folding pocket knife, which, though wiped down, still displayed traces of blood. The Hawk would verify its source. Local PD arrived to bring him in, but Warner and Olvida had to follow and file a brief report with the precinct captain before heading home. It took until mid-afternoon.

Entering their squad room, they were greeted by Special Agent Pauletti. "Ah, Detective, I was just looking for you." He joined Warner as he strolled toward his office.

"Out on a case, Lon." He glanced at the agent from the corner of his eye. "Whatcha got?"

"Our agents located Nick D'Amato."

Warner's brow wrinkled.

"The play's director."

"Oh, yeah. Ya find out where his people all dispersed to?" They entered his office and Warner waved Pauletti toward a chair as he settled in his own, forearms braced on it scarred surface.

"Not everyone, but he, the producer, and three actors, including both our persons of interest, Clive Warwick and Travis Mott, are all hanging out on South Beach."

"That's good. Both Warwick and Mott fit the profile, all right, but ..." He trailed off, eyes fastened on Pauletti.

"Yes, I know. Warwick seems almost *too* perfect, doesn't he?"

"Yeah." Warner slouched back and knuckled his eyes. "In my experience, of which I've had more'n I like the last few years, these guys are never easy." He surged back, hunkering over his desk and reached for his phone. "I'll send detectives out ta pick 'em up for Q & A."

"Not necessary." Pauletti gave a small wave. "I've dispatched agents from the Miami Field Office to find them and bring them here tomorrow, first thing. Give us a chance to question them individually and get DNA samples." He settled back in his chair, fingers interlaced across his belly. "I suspect you'll want your guy, Gold, to run the quick DNA tests. Be faster than sending them up to Quantico."

"Good. No disrespect, but ain't no one better'n the Hawk at this stuff." He paused and scratched his head. "Be nice ta tie this up now. Got the first of our juvie boot camp set for this weekend, and I don't wanna miss it, if I can avoid it."

"Oh yeah, I remember those from a few years back." Pauletti rose. "You and four other detectives, right?"

Warner nodded. "This is the fifth year. Been pretty successful, too." He also shoved to his feet and moved around his desk. "We've each continued ta mentor a couple of kids from past camps." He grinned. "My first is graduatin' college next year with a BA in business management." He patted Pauletti on the shoulder as they strolled from his office.

"He's a kid who may never have made it ta twenty until he attended our camp. I'm sorta the dad he never had in his life. We usually talk more'n once a month now."

"Really nice thing you started, Al." Pauletti pivoted to face him.

"Yeah, well, we keep some of 'em off the streets and give 'em purpose, then those are mugs we ain't gotta arrest later." He grunted. "Funny thing. It's usually the ones most rebellious at first who end up makin' the biggest change."

Pauletti nodded and started for the conference room to join his team. "Makes perfect sense. They're often the brightest." He patted Warner's arm. "So, I'll let you know, soon as we pick up everybody in the morning."

"Right. I'll see the Hawk is ready with everything he needs fer the samples, ready ta go. He's gonna be as eager as us ta nail this bastard."

With a wave, each man headed off on his own mission.

~ 32 ~

Warner hunched over his desk, reviewing the Baines crime scene report for the umpteenth time. With five members of the play's cast coming in that morning, he wanted to be sure he'd missed nothing as he readied for their interrogation. The plan was to set them at ease before requesting samples of their DNA.

He slouched back and glanced at his watch: 7:00 a.m. Too restless to sleep, he'd risen before dawn, out for a run with Buff to burn off tension, running a doubled route at a picked-up pace. More of a run than a jog, knowing he'd need to be extra fit the first session of this year's Juvi rehab weekend, their DCBC, scheduled to kick off on Friday. Four days 'til then to solve this mystery, or be once again dead in the water. The Hawk would have the quick DNA results by Wednesday afternoon, if all the subjects complied.

By the time he'd returned home, sweaty but calmer, Eva had breakfast on the table, so he'd showered, shaved, dressed, and after eating, spent twenty minutes with Andrea before hastening into the office. Playtime with his munchkin always seemed to calm his soul.

He glanced up as Jack Harris materialized in his doorway.

"Just heard from Agent Pauletti, Boss."

"And ...?"

"Agents from the Miami field office have corralled all five persons of interest, and they're on the way in." He chuckled. "Said they were a bit grumpy at the early hour, but the agents wanted to be sure they had them all before they got off on some business of their own."

"No trouble locatin' 'em, Jack?"

"Nah. All staying in the same boutique hotel on the beach. I forget which one." He settled on one of Warner's chairs. "How we gonna handle this, Boss? You doing the Q and A, or the Fibbies?"

"Me and Pauletti, I guess, and maybe Agent Whitehead. He's their top profiler." Arms raised, he stretched. "We'll go easy and non-confrontational. Settle 'em in the conference room—"

"Not an interrogation room," Harris cut in, eyebrows arched.

"Nah." Warner slouched back in his chair. "I want it non-confrontational. Keep 'em relaxed while we explain about the murders, and that we're queryin' anyone known ta be in the vicinity at the time." He sat up and shoved aside the file he'd been reading. "Tell 'em our askin' fer DNA samples are just normal procedure."

"They're gonna know we've got a crime scene sample to match it against, don't you think?"

"Yeah, probably, but we'll try ta keep it low key."

"And if they decline to give a sample?" Harris's hand rubbed the nape of his neck. "What then?"

"The ADA couldn't get warrants. Not enough probable cause, so we'll have ta figure somethin' else out," he said as they strode out, heading for the CSU lab to be sure the Hawk was teed up. "You see the conference room is set." He glanced again at his watch. "Pauletti give ya an ETA?"

"Between nine and nine-thirty," said as he glanced at a text on his phone. "Apparently Warwick was already out of his room, so they're tracking him down. Probably having breakfast." His phone pocketed, Harris headed for the conference room. “I’ll get a pot of coffee going. Maybe a backup way to get DNA.”

“Good idea. A box of donuts, too. The rest of the BAU team will have to move out into the bullpen to make room.”

“Copy that,” Harris said.

Warner shot back over his shoulder as he reached the exit, “I’ll see The Hawk has all his supplies up there, ready for the samplin’.”

I got a good feelin’ we’re gonna end this bastard, right here, right now.

He hurried on to the forensic lab to set it up.

Detective Harris pushed through the double doors of the forensic lab and spied Warner talking with Moe Gold, the Hawk.

“So, yer gonna bring it all with you in that tray, huh?”

“Yes, Detective. I have to keep it always in my control to verify nothing has been tampered with.” The little CSU whiz ran a protective hand over the vials and swabs nestled in a segmented box. “This way, if we *do* find our perp’s DNA, no one can challenge it’s chain of custody in court.”

“Gotcha.” Warner’s head pivoted at Harris’s approach. “Ready, Jack?”

“Yep. All five arrived about four minutes ago.”

“Anybody goin’ for the coffee or donuts? In case they refuse to give DNA.” He started for the doorway.

“None that I saw, Boss.” Harris turned to follow. “Couple of them mentioned they’d just finished breakfast.”

Warner chuckled. “As good a dodge as any. I guess.” They were out the door and headed for the squad room. “The CCTV cameras will spot anyone usin’ a cup, and we can retrieve it later.” Warner paused as they entered the bullpen. “Let ’em sit a while before we go in.” He gave Harris a gentle shove. “Find Agent Pauletti and ask him ta wait fer me. We’ll go in together." A glance at his watch. "Say ten minutes."

"Gotcha, Boss. I'll tee up the agent." He stopped. "Want me to come by when it's time to go?"

Warner nodded. "Meanwhile, I'm gonna revisit our two Persons of Interest's files so I got all their background straight." He turned toward his office. "Ya know where ta find me, buddy."

A soft rap on his doorjamb drew Warner's eyes from the paper he was studying.

"Ready, Boss?" Jack Harris stood in the opening.

"Yeah, let's do this." He rose and came out from behind his desk. "Pauletti on tap?"

Harris nodded. "With Agent Whitehead in tow."

"Good move. He's their top profiler. Aughta be able ta read the room."

Harris nodded. "The Hawk's coming up, but you said you didn't want him to be there until you called him in."

"Right." They strode together toward the BAU Agents, who were lingering just outside the conference room. "Wanna do the Q & A before they get nervous about givin' up DNA." They joined the two federal agents. "Ready?"

Both nodded, so Warner entered the room, his team trailing. He found the five cast members all in chairs. No foam coffee cups donut remnants sat on the table, so they would have to rely on voluntary submission of DNA. A suspect can't be forced to give it up without a warrant, and they'd struck out there.

Three of the men rose as Warner's team entered. A middle-age, paunchy guy, gray streaked auburn haired, probably early fifties, stepped forward, hand extended.

"You're Detective Warner?"

Warner nodded, taking his hand, and noted he was too

short to be their perp.

"I'm Nick D'Amato, director of *A Murder Mystery.*" He waved at his four associates. "Clive Warwick, Travis Mott, and Clara Bono are all part of the cast, and that good looking guy on the end is Tony Ryder, our producer." Each waved or nodded at the mention of their name. "I understand this is related to a murder investigation that you somehow think one of us may be involved with?"

"No one's a suspect in anything at this point." Warner studied the four men, settled back in their seats, as he perched on the corner of the large, oval oak table. "Right now, we're just collectin' information." The three guys, other than D'Amato, were each about right height and build to be their perp.

"So, why the interest in my group?" D'Amato leaned back, fingers intertwined over his bulge.

"Frankly, 'cause we're trackin' a serial killer." Warner folded his arms across his chest. "We've IDed him as a travelin' guy who tends ta follow a route throughout the South and the Southeast, killin' an attractive, black-haired woman in each city." He paused and scanned the crowd, but saw nothing more than peaked interest. A glance at Agent Whitehead drew a bare shrug. "Coincidentally, your play was performing in each city for every murder. Eighteen times!" He shrugged. "And no good cop believes in coincidences, as you know from your play's script."

This created a stir among the five. "Wow! Eighteen victims? And you've read our script?" D'Amato asked.

"Saw the play with my wife, actually, when you were in Miami two years ago." He chuckled. "She dragged me for a night out, fer a break on a case I was workin'." He chuckled. "Liked it, ta my surprise, and was pleasantly astonished at how much ya got right."

"And you think one of us may be this killer?" Clive Warwick piped up.

"Just coverin' our bases, Mr. Warwick. As you must know from the research the play-writer probably did, an investigation is mostly about eliminations, which, hopefully, lead ta the real perp." He pushed to his feet. "That's what we're doin' here. Tryin' ta thin out the suspect pool."

"And that pool includes us? Do you have anything you think may connect *any* of us?" Tony Ryder asked. "Any plausible motive?" His elbows rested on the table, chin cupped in his hands,

"We're digging into all of that," Pauletti pitched in. "Agent Whitehead here, and I, are with the FBI's BAU, and we've worked with Detective Warner before on these kinds of cases, so we're here to help find the killer. Just so you know, we're researching the lives and social media histories of every member of your crew, cast and support staff."

Warner and the Fibbies studied the group, searching for any physical response to that. All fidgeted restlessly, not unexpected under the circumstances.

"Behavioral specialist, right?" Travis Mott asked after a moment of silence, squirming in his chair.

"Yes," Whitehead responded, "but only to assist the detective. Through years of collaborations, we've learned he's top notch at this." He paused. "This is a multifaceted operation. Serial killers are rarely easily caught, and many actually are never brought to justice. I'm sure you know the many famous cases that were never solved."

"So, does anyone have anything ta say? Any ideas about how these murders were committed when your play was always in town?" He paused. "Or by whom, if something comes ta ya."

This was met with universally mumbled dissent and head shakes.

"Nothin', huh?" Warner shrugged. "Okay. Well, one more thing then, before we let ya get back ta yer vacations."

He stepped to the door and opened it, revealing the Hawk, bearing a honeycomb metal tray with five upright vials and swabbing supplies.

"Just as a matter of procedure, we'd like to get DNA samples from all yer group. The five of ya are here, so we can get yours now."

"You have DNA from the killer?" Warwick asked.

"Possibly." He drew the Hawk in, who set his things on the table, his intense dark eyes sweeping the five people.

"We got somthin', but ain't sure if it's the killer's or someone else's." He patted his short tech chief on the shoulder. "Just part of the elimination we talked about earlier." Warner scanned their faces. "Anyone got a problem with givin' a DNA sample?"

"Do you have warrants for this, Detective?" Travis Mott rose, hands on his hips.

"Do I need one for you ta give me a sample, Mr. Mott?"

"As a matter of fact, yes." Mott looked at the other four. "I don't know about you guys, but without a warrant, it's voluntary, and frankly, I'm not crazy about having my DNA out where it may be exploited."

"We don't publish it, sir," the Hawk said. "It's solely for our internal use."

"So you say, but I still don't like it." He plucked his light jacket off the back of his chair and moved toward the door. "If that's it for now, I'm leaving." He glanced at his companions. "What about it, guys?"

Nick D'Amato shrugged and looked around. "I got no problem giving them my DNA. Clears me of any involvement, and that's a better outcome, as far as I'm concerned."

This was met with nods and mumbled accents by the other four.

"Okay. I drove up here alone, so I'm outta here." Mott gave a small wave. "See you back at the hotel." And he was out the door.

Warner's eyes followed his exit. *Wasn't originally at the top of my suspect list, but that's changed now.* He swung back to the rest of the party.

"Okay, this is easy and fast. The Hawk," nodding at his forensic ace who had gathered up a fistful of sterile cotton swabs, "will take saliva samples from yer mouths. Easy and painless. You'll be free ta go inside of ten minutes."

Moe Gold, the Hawk, stepped forward. "Who's first?"

Clive Warwick stood and held out a hand. "I'll do it myself." He gestured at the swabs.

"What?" The Hawk's brow wrinkled. "I need to maintain security of the specimens, so I don't think—"

"We discussed this earlier among ourselves," Warwick stood hands on hips. "We were expecting this might be coming, and we'd all like to swab our own cheeks, if you don't mind." He studied Warner. "It's not that complicated, and you can watch to see we get it right, but it *is* voluntary, and we're more comfortable this way."

Warner looked at the Hawk. "Moe?"

"I guess it's okay, Detective. Pretty hard to screw this up." He handed a swab to Warwick. "Rotate the cotton tip against your inner cheek. Just don't let the cotton touch anything else until it goes into one of these sealed tubes."

"Got it." He reached for a swab. Ten minutes later, with four samples encased in sterile vials, the four people were on their way back to South Beach and the rest of their vacation.

The Hawk would run a quick DNA test and get preliminary results the next day. If any suspected match was discovered, a more traditional, extensive test would be conducted to verify the results. Warner retired to his office, where two more murders awaited his attention. One, committed by an illegal Haitian immigrant, had already been solved, and Detectives Dean and Salinas were tracking down the perp.

Always plenty to keep Miami-Dade Homicide busy.

~~~

Warner entered the CSU lab the next afternoon and spotted the Hawk, hunched over a microscope. He stepped over and noted the man was comparing two bullets through the device. He hunkered there for a moment, awaiting the tech's attention, then finally spoke up.

"Got those DNA matches finished yet, Moe." He waited, hands in his pockets, as his little genius continued to stare into the scope's eyepiece.

"In a minute, Detective. I know you're there." He made a small adjustment to a dial, then grunted. "Ha! Gotcha." He straightened and rotated on his swivel stool. "Just got the match on the bullet from the gun used on the Haitian's victim." He slipped off his seat and waved Warner to follow as he headed for his desk. "Both from the same Ruger .32. That'll tie up that case for Detective Beck." He settled at his desk and pawed through a small stack of papers.

"I finished the DNA results for the four who agreed, and I've got them ... ah, here." He withdrew a small packet of paper, clipped together. "Was just about to call you when the bullet came in from autopsy, and Detective Beck was on my tail for a result." He leafed through the four pages. "So, here's the upshots. Sorry to say, I couldn't find a match to our killer."

"Really?" Warner rubbed the back of his neck. "I was pretty confident one of those two guys was our perp, though only Warwick readily agreed to the DNA tests."

"But the other wouldn't give a sample. Mott, right?" The little man shifted back in his chair. "You think it's him, then?"

"Don't know." Warner sighed. "Agent Pauletti's team did a preliminary dive inta his social media, but apparently
~~~

it was pretty slim. Not very active on Facebook, X, or any of the usual places. Still workin' on pullin' a more complete history, but that'll take a while."

"How about other cast members who aren't in the Miami area?"

"The BAU's diggin', but it'll take a while ta get a full history on everyone else who might fit the physical description, height and build-wise."

"Well, like you said, these guys are never easy." He pushed back and rose, handing Warner the sheaf of papers. "Meanwhile, I'll run a more complete DNA test to be sure the fast results didn't miss anything. And I think I'll also run them through the national data base."

"Good idea. Maybe ya'll get a hit on something that ties inta our case, anyhow." Warner rubbed the back of his neck. "Looks like we're back ta the drawin' board. Keep me posted if ya turn up anything useful, Moe."

"Count on that, Detective."

Said to Warner's back as he was already exiting the room. His thoughts flitted to the coming weekend and the twenty-eight juvie delinquents they were going to try to give a reason to leave the gangs.

They always presented a challenge, but it was worth the effort if they could save just a few of them.

~ 33 ~

He slumped in the driver's seat of his Equinox and watched the other three drive off together in D'Amato's Chrysler. He made an angry shake of his head. *Sloppy, sloppy, sloppy! Musta dripped some semen when I flushed the condom.* No other way they'd have DNA.

If they actually *did* have it. He'd been so scrupulous over the years, even bringing a small porta-vac for the sheets and any place he may have sat.

With a grunt, he fired up the SUV's engine, but continued to linger in PARK. *Lucky we'd decided to ask to do the DNA swabs ourselves.* He'd been unsure if they would allow that, but after some discussion, and a gentle lead from him, they' agreed if they weren't allowed to self-swab, they'd all refuse to comply. Clearly, the cops didn't have enough for subpoenas, or there'd never have been an "ask."

He chuckled, then reached inside his mouth and winced slightly as he detached the tiny glass tube he'd Superglued to the inside of his cheek. He studied it as the tip of his tongue explored the small sore removing it had created. His lips curled into a gentle smile as the tube was slipped into a breast pocket.

A soft sigh filled the interior of the car as he began toward Miami Beach. Once they were summoned for a next morning visit to police HQ, he'd visited the hotel's bar that evening and picked up a drink glass used by a rather squirrelly looking guy. He'd been entrusted with the cast's makeup case for storage until next season, and using the tools therein, managed to extract a good sample from the glass's rim and secure it inside a small vial with a slit rubber seal. He'd made several practice runs at putting a swap into his mouth, avoiding any contact with his actual cheek or tongue, while pushing the cotton tip through the slit top. Swirling it around, he then withdrew it, again avoiding collecting *his* DNA. He'd been confident if the cops wanted DNA, he could pull it off.

And he had, sure that the swab came out clean, without touching any of his own mouth. The FBI's Behavioral Analysis Unit had surely done a deep background check and thought they had their man. They were going to be disappointed, but somehow, they'd put together that the vigilante killing those wicked, heartless women was a member of their show. Someone had the epiphany, and they certainly were able to track the play's schedule. And, presto, there they were, in town for all eighteen murders, before he'd taken lovely Courtney here, with no performance scheduled.

Of course, we are here ... the five of us, and those talented BAU profilers had undoubtedly found more than one likely culprit among us. So, did they have anything besides DNA and a social history that might ID their prey? He couldn't imagine what.

He sighed. What to do next? Another black-haired bitch had surfaced at a beachfront bistro twice over the last three days. Surely a heartless woman needing punishment. Two things about that, though, screamed for control. First, she'd seen him as he was and not in one of his many disguises. And more important, this local cop. Warner, had an amazing record at catching people like him. Once he'd learned of the coming Q & A at Miami Police HQ, he'd Googled Detective Al Warner. Six serial killers caught over the last six years, one of which had confounded the FBI for two decades. So, a super cop, not someone to give a bone. Another round of punishment so soon after the wicked Courtney Baines would be too great a risk, no matter how deserving she was.

Was it time to boogie? He'd staked out a small cabin, deep in a tiny, hidden vale of the Blue Ridge Mountains, already fully stocked for a protracted stay. Despite its seclusion, it had Skylink Wi-Fi service. The closest small town was an hour's drive over a rutted, often overgrown lane. He could manage a year back there, and even arrange for visits to a dark web clinic where he could achieve a complete physical makeover. He'd have to resist venturing into nearby cities, seeking sinners in need of punishment though. If he needed to hide out, no sense in leaving a scent for the FBI dogs ... or Detective Al Warner.

He shook his head and grunted as he pulled into his hotel's parking lot and prepaid for the night. Nothing free in Miami Beach. Parked, he exited the Chevy and started for the rear door. Not yet a good time to run ... unless he feared they'd somehow ID him. Better to hang in there, lay low, and enjoy the beach. Plenty of hot, young babes for conventional sex to keep him busy, and he *did* love fucking a sexy, young woman.

An image of this newest black-haired witch bloomed in his mind, perched at the bar, eying him with a sidewise glance, a tempting smile tilting her lips. He gritted his teeth, knowing she lusted to dominate him, unaware of the punishment she'd get for her lascivious desire.

But he couldn't do it, with the cops breathing down his neck. Quell the desire to stick it in their face.

No time for an ego trip. He'd let this one get away, but would rue the damage she'd surely do to someone else. Someone unable to fight back.

That wasn't him.

Not anymore.

~ 34 ~

Warner's Charger bounced and swayed as he drove north on the dirt path, searching the heavy Everglades growth for the sign. A glance at his odometer showed he ventured a bit more than three miles from Alligator Alley, so it should be close ...

There! Partially obscured by sawgrass: "BOOT CAMP." He turned right into an even more rugged path, stopped, exited his coupe with a machete, and hacked away the grass so the sign would be more visible. Not going to give these delinquents any excuse about missing the turnoff.

"If Hector's already here," he mumbled, "he shoulda cleared that away." Back in his Dodge, he continued up the lane, the bottom of the low-slung car often dragging over growth on the overgrown path. *First chore for the kids is gonna be ta clear this off.* After two-hundred-yards, he broke into an open glade and spotted Hector's Dodge Ram, Franklin's F-150, and Ellison's Hummer, parked together at the far end of the meadow. Apparently, Jorge Ignacio was yet to arrive in his Toyota Tundra, probably delayed in picking up the food and portable cooking and cooling devices.

Warner stepped from his vehicle, immediately attacked by blood-hungry mosquitos and sticky heat from the mid-afternoon sun. He spied his three detective friends in the process of raising a second sleeping tent, with one already erected along a side of the clearing. The open dining tent and its framework lay on the ground in the middle glade, awaiting their attention.

"Hey, guys." Warner strode toward the two men. "Ya got a good start." He nodded at the entry lane. "I cleared the growth away from the road sign. Figured ya were more intent on gettin' the site set up." He snatched up a mallet, grabbed a rope to straighten the last pole, and pounded the stake into the soft earth, completing the final erecting of the tent.

"Heard from Jorge?" He mopped his brow, sweating from midday heat, the sun still high in a cloudless, azure sky.

"On the way," Ellison said. "Should arrive within thirty." He turned toward his Hummer. "I gotta get the genny set up now for the coolers, and we gotta string lights."

"Okay," Warner responded. He swatted a mosquito on his neck and turned to Hector Carrera. "Got any bug spray?"

"Don't come into the 'Glades without it, pal," said as he withdrew a can of Deep Woods OFF from his cargo pocket and tossed it to Warner.

"Thanks." Warner sprayed his neck and arms, then the palms of his hands, which he rubbed on his face. "Left mine in the car.

"So, let's finish what we can before Jorge gets here. The kids aughta start arriving in less than three hours." Hector strode toward the F-150 which held most of the folding cots.

Two hours later, Detective Jorge Ignacio had arrived, and the camp site was fully operational. Soon after, the first of their charges filed in, and the rest trickled in over the next forty minutes. As per instructions, they were delivered by adults and left sans any vehicles and cell phones. They' were allowed no path to leave early, and no electronics to cause distractions. The next forty-eight hours would be spent on physical exertion and classwork, and no one was allowed to shirk. Goofing off or insurrection was dealt with nothing more physical than a mile run through the 'Glades, always led by Darnell Franklin. The black, past all-state running back detective booked no nonsense, and none of their charges, who were mostly black and Hispanic, could claim racial persecution.

Forty-eight hours later, Warner lingered in his Charger as he watched the last of the boys leave, just after seven p.m., Sunday evening. He groaned, tired and a smidge achy after a busy, physical two days. He glanced around the camp site, which would remain standing over the next three weeks until they'd complete the four-session boot camp. Park rangers would stop by at least daily to see everything was left undisturbed.

He was pleased that only five rebels had surfaced, and one of them seemed to be coming around by the end of the third day. About half the kids really got into the camping vibe, and most of the rest took a wait-and-see attitude. The boys all learned that these five cops each came from underprivileged backgrounds, just like them: Warner with an abusive father from rural, northern Illinois; Carrera and Ignacio from families escaping the brutality of Castro's Cuba; Ellison from hard-scrabble, cracker farmers, south of Orlando; and Franklin from a fatherless family, right there in Overtown. Each had benefited from men who saw them for something more than delinquents, providing the positive male influence all boys need.

He sighed, and fired up his engine. Time to get back to civilization. He had a serial killer to catch, and without the expected DNA hit on his two persons of interest, they were back to page one. He glanced at the dashboard clock, seeing he'd be home in time for some play with his daughter. And usually, Adele baked peach turnovers, his favorites, for his returns from the weekends. Then his lovely redhead would drain away any residual tensions with gentle but passionate loving.

He fidgeted on the car's seat in anticipation of that. Then, Monday was back to the hunt. DNA match or not, they still had a killer to catch, and Warner's very reliable "gut" told him it was one of the play's crew. They were missing something.

He needed to figure out what that was.

~ 35 ~

Warner tip-toed from the bedroom and eased the door closed. It was 5:40 a.m., and he didn't want to disturb Eva. They'd spent nearly two hours the previous evening slaking passion. Her first, then him, followed a bit later by a slower, more tender encore. But now she needed to sleep, with a full schedule of troubled clients, many of them cops, on her plate for the coming day. Fielding all their emotional discharge would bring her home wrung out.

He tiptoed to the guest bathroom where he'd left his jogging outfit: denim cargo shorts, a Miami Heat t-shirt, and a ball cap. He studied himself in the mirror, and fingers traced scars, two from bullets creasing his head, and the other a knife wound. He smiled and chuffed softly. *Still pretty ripped for an old fart. Well, maybe not old, but on the far side of forty.*

His small weightroom in the garage was religiously visited, filling a need to be fit. *Two slugs off the identical spot on my hard noggin ain't gonna slow me down, if I got somethin' ta say about it.*

He swiveled at the sound of nailed paws clacking softly on the tile and spotted Buff, sitting in the doorway, head cocked, warm, brown eyes regarding him quizzically.

"All good, bud?" he whispered, crouching and scratched behind the dog's furry ears. "Ya kept Andy safe another night, huh?"

The golden retriever seemed to nod, then licked his cheek. The big animal had taken to sleeping outside their daughter's bedroom at night, ever since that lunatic assassin attacked both Eva and the baby. Warner had no doubt that gentle dog would become a furious missile if someone tried that again.

"Okay, pal. Let me dress, and we'll go for a run." He glanced down at the still sitting animal. "Ya got two miles in ya today? I gotta burn off some tension before goin' ta work."

The dog gave a quiet chuff, rose, and headed for their front door.

"I swear that pup understands everything I say ta him," Warner muttered as he tied his sneakers, pocketed his compact 9mm S & W ankle gun, and picked up his keys. He never ran unprotected anymore. Too many crazies out there. He strode to the door and canceled then reset the alarm, hoping the beeps didn't disturb Eva. He'd silenced the "Open Door" alarms the evening before, just for that purpose. He had thirty-seconds to get out and close the door before the alarm reset. Keeping his family safe was a priority.

"Buff. Heel," and he was out the door, which he relocked, his furry buddy at his side. They'd complete the run with Buff at heel most of the route, only releasing him to "do his business." Warner had pocketed several plastic bags for that very purpose.

The golden rim of the Sun edged above a horizon of low rooftops, casting long shadows as Warner accelerated into a sprint across the last two-hundred-yards, Buff loping easily at his side. Slowed to a trot at the end, he paused at the stoop of his townhouse to catch his breath and check his pulse. With a resting heart rate in the mid-forties, he rarely could push it above 120, and despite the hard run, that day was no exception. He squatted and the dog sat at his side in proper heel mode. Warner's arms circled his neck and drew him in for a hug, his face receiving a thorough tongue-washing.

"I love ya too, buddy." He rose, gave the animal an ear-scratching, then picked up Adele's *Miami Herald* from the walk, and placed it at his neighbor's front door. While still spry at 92, he always tried to save her steps. Back to his home, he entered through the garage and deposited a well-filled bag of dog poop in the trash. Buff followed him into the house and immediately went to Andrea's door for a few sniffs. Finding nothing amiss, he padded to his water bowl for a healthy drink, then settled on his bed to watch his hero, the man who saved his life, begin to prepare breakfast.

Warner turned at the creak of an opening door and spied Eva, clad in one of his khaki, shirts, its sleeve rolled up past her elbows, the tail at mid-thigh. She ran fingers through tousled auburn hair, a grin twitching up the corners of her lips.

"Mmm. The aroma of coffee and bacon. Smells yummy." She sidled next to him and bussed his cheek. "Doing my morning chores, are you?"

"Yeah, well, I was up early for a two-mile run with the pup and thought I'd let ya sleep in fer a change. Still pretty early."

"Thanks, hon. I've got a full schedule today, so this early start is nice." She poured two cups of coffee, both black, and set them on the table. "You peek in on Andrea?"

"Yeah. Buff already checked her out, and she's still asleep."

Eva perched on a chair and sipped her coffee, her emerald eyes fastened on her husband. "You had a restless night, Al. I know you've had a lot going on—"

He nodded. "A big spate of local murders and drive-bys, but I'm really miffed at lack of progress on our new serial killer." He plated eggs-over-easy, and three strips of crisp bacon on two dishes. Adele-baked buttermilk biscuits from the toaster oven were added, and he set breakfast on the table.

"I thought you had a solid person of interest." Eva separated her biscuit and cut into the egg, sopping up the runny yellow with the warm dough.

"We do." He settled across from her and began to eat. "Unfortunately, the DNA didn't match on one of them, and the other refused to give a sample." He grunted. "Said it made him uncomfortable to have it 'out there.'"

"Not an unreasonable thought. I can see someone not wanting to have their DNA out in cyberspace for someone to manipulate with AI."

"Yeah, but—"

"Yes, I know. You keep it in house, with no public access, but *he* doesn't know that. At least, not for sure." Finished eating, she dabbed her lips with a napkin. "Good breakfast, lover." Eased back in her chair, she sipped her coffee. "So, what's next?"

"Keep diggin', I guess." He inhaled the last of the biscuit and gazed at his wife.

"I'm sure it's someone in that play's crew, and with this Trevor Mott rufusin' to give DNA, he's become suspect numero uno, but something still doesn't sit right with that." Rising, he gathered their dishes and set them in the sink.

"You shower and dress, Al." Eva also stood. "I've got some time, with this early breakfast, so I'll clean up and check on the imp." She cocked her head. "In fact, sounds like she's awake." She watched Buff pad to the baby's door and sit. "Looks like her sentry thinks so too."

They both chuckled, and Warner stepped over and ruffled the big dog's fur. "Good boy, Buff." Then he headed for the bedroom, stripping off his shirt as he went. "I sure can use that shower."

Warner sat on his bed, slipping on his shoes, when his cell phone vibrated. He snatched it up and hit the green light.

"Warner." Then put the phone on speaker, laying it on the bed beside him as he finished donning his shoes.

"Good morning, Detective," the Hawk said. "I hope I didn't wake you, but I know you're up early and—"

"Ya got somthin' good, Moe? I'm just gettin' ready ta leave."

"Not sure if it's good, Al, but it's interesting. Come see me in the lab when you arrive."

"Yer not gonna tell me what ya got until I get there, are ya?"

"Better if I show you, Detective. Frankly, I'm a bit confounded by this whole thing."

"Great! Now yer makin' me crazy." Phone in hand, he holstered his Glock in his shoulder rig and shrugged on a light jacket. "I'll be there in thirty. Ya want anyone else."

"Whomever you think appropriate on the serial killer case. Surely Pauletti and some of his team, and maybe Detectives Harris and Olvida."

"Right. You contact Harris and he'll corral everyone." Phone in hand, he strode into the kitchen for a brief kiss for Eva and a hug and kiss from Andy, now in her booster chair. A moment later, he was in the garage, the door rolling up as he slipped into his Charger. "Like I said, a half hour, and don't start without me." He set the cell into its holder on the dash.

"I'm wounded, AL." A soft chuckle. "You know, you're *always* my first go-to."

"Yeah, yeah." He'd backed out, the door rumbling down as he sped away.

"See ya soon. I hope it's good, but I'll take anything right now." He disconnected and resisted using his siren and lights. Whatever the Hawk found wasn't going away, if he took a few extra minutes getting there and managed to arrive alive.

Miami's traffic was brutal.

Warner parked his gunmetal gray coupe into his reserved spot, killed the engine, and stepped out. He paused, and squinting against shimmering beams from the just rising sun, scanned the still mostly vacant lot. Harris's and Olvida's cars sat in their respective spots, and two black Chevy Suburban's, preferred Fed vehicles, occupied guest spots. Not yet 7:00 a.m., but they all lived, or rented in the case of the BAU, closer than he. He nodded approval and trotted toward HQ's entrance, eager to learn what the Hawk had discovered. "Interesting," he'd said, but not necessarily probative.

Inside the building, he headed for the forensic lab where he spied his two lead detectives and Agents Pauletti, Yeager, and Askin awaiting his arrival. They turned to greet him.

"The Hawk said to wait for you, Boss," Harris said. "He wouldn't show us anything 'til you arrived. Said he promised you."

"Yeah, well, I like ta be in at the top, but I think he carried it too far." He shoved open the door. "Anyway, let's see what he's come up with." Warner scanned the room as he entered and spied the Hawk at his desk, studying a file.

"So, Moe, whatcha got that's so interestin'?" He halted in front of the desk, arms folded, as the smaller man looked up, a tiny grin creasing his lips.

"Strange stuff, Detective." He rose and offered Warner the filed he'd been reading. "As you know, the preliminary DNA samples showed no match for anyone to our killer, so I ran them through CODIS, and what do you know, I got a hit."

"For our perp?" Warner flipped open the file and scanned the first page.

"Strangely, no, but one of them *was* a match for a wanted child molester in Virginia. One Ricardo Lopes Macha." The Hawk gave a wry chuckle, and looked at Pauletti. "No resemblance to any of our suspects, but you should check his history and see if that matches up with any of the crime scenes." He paused. "But there's something else about that sample I've got to dig more deeply into."

"What, Moe?" Warner's brow wrinkled. "None of this makes sense."

"I don't want to say, Detective, until I've had a chance to verify my concerns. I don't want to start you off on what may be just a wild goose chase."

"Ah, c'mon, I don't wanna waste—"

"Yes, I know you're eager to make the collar, but I've got my process, and even *you* can't rush me." He took the file from Warner. "A day or two, at most. Be patient," chuckling, "something you've yet to learn, Al."

"Okay. Yer who ya are, and I ain't gonna change that." He gestured at the file. "Meanwhile, make copies of that and we'll dig inta this child molesting case. See if there's any connection. Don't make sense, but we can't let it slide."

"Right. I'll get the Bureau checking his history," Pauletti said. "See if it ties him to any of this. Meanwhile, we still have two persons of interest to follow up here."

"Yeah, and this guy, Travis Mott, never gave DNA samples, so he needs a real scrubbin'."

"We'll do that too, Al. May take a day or two, at most."

"Yeah, well, I'm getting' damned tired of waitin'. This perp's killed once already, unconnected to the play. I wanna get him before he tries it again."

With murmured assent from all, the five left the room,

each on their own mission.

~ 36 ~

Chief of Detectives, Al Warner, perched at his desk as he poured over a recent After-Action report. Detective Salinas, while investigating a recent Cuban Cartel assassination, was drawn into a shootout at a liquor store. The two perps who attempted the strong-arm robbery apparently never noticed the detective and two patrol cops a few hundred feet up the street, questioning local Latinos about the killing. One robber died at the scene and the other was a U of Miami hospital trauma center in critical condition. One of the patrol cops took a 9mm in the shoulder, but had already been discharged from care.

As was often the case after discharging a weapon, Salinas was on temporary leave while it was investigated to verify the shooting was justified. Which no one questioned that, they had to go through "procedure." Warner suspected Salinas would be back on the Job withing the week.

He eased back in his chair as Detective Harris and Agent Pauletti appeared in his doorway, and he waved them in. They entered, sat in front of his desk, and Paoletti plopped a thickish file on his desk.

"What's this?" Warner plucking up the file.

"The considerable rap sheet of Ricardo Macha." Pauletti leaned back, fingers interlocked across his belly.

"Macha?" Warner's brow wrinkled. "Oh, yeah, the child molester whose DNA showed up in our samplin'." The file flipped open, Warner eyed the photo: rough-shaven face, whisky-colored skin, and a cruel twist to his lips. Unusual gray eyes stared back at him. "Don't look much like a Romeo these gals woulda fallen fer, does he?"

"Yeah, Boss." Harris leaned forward. "But he fits the physical description: 5-11 and fit."

"Yeah, I see that. But how the fuck did we get his DNA from the play's crew?" He flipped pages. "Jesus, he's sure got the history fer it. Attempted rape, maybe murder, lots of unproven allegations fer all kinda violence, both kids and women." His eyes found Pauletti's. "How the hell is he still skatin' free?"

"Lots of conundrums there, Detective," Pauletti said. "Some of his charges were interstate, so we've got jurisdiction, but the larger unanswered question is the one you first asked: how did his DNA get into the mix with the ones we took from those five people?"

"Don't know." Warner stood. "Maybe the Hawk'll have an answer for that. He said somethin' was botherin' him about this particular sample, so we'll see what he comes up with." He hauled Harris from his chair and headed out his door, Pauletti close behind. He handed Harris Macha's rap sheet.

"Meanwhile, we got a guy who need's catchin', right here in Miami Beach. There are three warrants for his arrest in there, Jack. Get tech on the hotel where the actors were stayin' ta survey their CCTVs. Let's put this nasty puppy away."

"On it, Boss," and the detective hurried off, headed for the Tech Department.

Warner turned to Pauletti. "I'm headin' down ta see the Hawk. Maybe he's found somethin'. Wanna come?"

"Glad to. Got nothing else viable to work on at the moment." They exited the Detectives Department together.

Warner pushed through the swinging doors, Pauletti on his heels, and his nose wrinkled. The smell of formaldehyde and exploded gunshots hung in the air. He spied the Hawk at a table, just removing a handgun from the bullet collection rack, the apparent reason for the gunpowder odor.

"Ah, Detective." The little man waved at seeing Warner. "I was about to call you." He ejected the magazine from the 9mm Beretta he'd just fired, and jacked out the slug still in the chamber, inserting it back into the magazine. He brandished the weapon. "Detective Salinas's weapon. Getting bullets for a match from his recent shooting for the review board.

"Right." Warner paused, hands on hips. "It was a righteous shoot. Just reviewed the A.R., and it was by the book. Need ta get him cleared and back on duty, ASAP."

"I'll have these processed in an hour and get them up to the board. It was his gun that killed one of the shooters, so I'll do the match. Shouldn't be a problem."

"So." Warner shrugged. "You were gonna call me, Moe?"

"Yes. About those DNA samples."

"Yeah." Warner plopped onto a seat, Pauletti standing behind. "DNA from a pretty bad guy, who could fit as our serial killer, except he wasn't in the room, swabbin' his cheek." He stared at the CSA tech. "Ya come up with a reason fer that?"

"Possibly." He settled behind his cluttered desk, sorting through papers and apparently finding what he sought. He held the paper up and shook it.

"Here's the results of that test."

"Who's was it?" Warner plucked it from the man's fingers.

"Unfortunately, of that I'm uncertain. Somehow, the collection notes got scrambled. It's one of three men, but I'm unsure which one." He leaned forward, elbows resting on his desk. "What I *am* now sure of however, is that it's corrupted by other DNA."

Warner's eyebrows arched. "What d'ya mean, corrupted?" He lay the sheet back on the desk.

"If you read that," nodding at the report, "you'd see it was only a 90% match to the Macha guy."

"Ninety percent?" Warner glanced at Pauletti who'd picked up the report. "I don't understand."

"There was a small bit of other DNA in the batch, Al." He hesitated for a beat. "Apparently, DNA from someone else."

"Someone else? I don't get it. How's that possible?"

"I have no answer for that, but it's clear to me that one of our subjects had DNA, somehow collected from Mr. Macha, and was able to submit it instead of his own." The tech shrugged. "In the process, he contaminated it with a tiny bit of his, but not enough to make an ID, or even a suggestion."

Warner grunted. "So, what yer sayin' is, somehow, with us right there, watchin' 'em swab their cheeks, one of these guys was able to produce Macha's DNA while avoidin' samplin' his own ... mostly." He stared at the Hawk. "How's that possible?" he repeated.

"The only explanation is somehow he had an isolated sample of Macha's DNA on his inner cheek and swabbed that, and in the process, slightly contaminated it with a bit of his own." The short man shrugged. "Maybe some sort of vial stuck inside his cheek. Or whatever, he managed to pull it off." He pushed up from his desk. "The quick DNA results aren't as perfect as the longer ones, but there was enough there to cause me to look further. "That's what I found, Detective. It's up to you to figure out what to do with it."

"Yeah. Thanks a lot, buddy." Warner glanced at Pauletti. "We're gonna have ta get those people back in here and somehow get true DNA, or we got nothin'."

"Yes," the agent said, "Everything else—their proximity to each crime, their troubled backgrounds—are all circumstantial at best. No clear perpetrator at this moment."

They exited the lab together and were met by Detective Olvida in the corridor.

"I was just looking for you, Boss." He joined them en route to Detectives.

"What'cha got, Ralph?"

"A hit on Macha on South Beach. A CCTV picked him up, entering a boardwalk bar twenty-minutes ago."

"Weird turn of events." Warner hurried up the stairs, the other two close on his heels. "Someone, surely our serial nut, provides us the DNA of another perp while tryin' to disguise his own." He gave a wry chuckle. "And now we got a new case we can close on a totally different set of crimes." He looked at Olvida. "What'cha got workin', Ralph?

"Two Beach patrol cars, four blues, are on station, front and rear."

"With instructions not to engage unless he leaves, Ralph?"

"Yeah, of course." He chuckled. "Been with you long enough to know what you want here, Boss." He peeked at his watch. "About a fifteen-minute ride, if we leave now."

"Right. Harris, yer with me. Ralph, you pick up Dean." He touched Agent Pauletti's arm. "You want in on this, Lon?"

"Of course. There're federal warrants on him. I'll bring Agents Yeager and Whitehead." He looked at Detective Olvida. "Text me the address, and we'll meet you there."

"On it." He retrieved his phone and did the job as he got to his desk to get his shield and weapon.

Two-minutes later, two cars of Detectives, and the Fed's Chevy Suburban raced east toward the MacArthur Causeway and Miami Beach. At least, this was a case they could get their teeth into, and probably bring to a quick conclusion.

Warner hoped they could do it this time without any gunfire, but was glad Ina Yeager was joining them. She, and her big Barret .50, were great backup if there were violence.

The police radio squawked in Warner's car as he exited the MacArther Causeway into Miami Beach.

"Patrol Sargeant Evers for Detective Warner. You copy?"

Jack Harris grabbed the mic as Warner continued East toward South Beach.

"This is Harris with Warner. Got you, five-by-five. What's your sitrep?"

"Good copy, Detective. I've got one squad covering the rear of Waterway Cantina and two cars in front, awaiting your arrival, per instructions."

"Copy." Harris glanced at Warner, who nodded. "Should be on site in about five. Any visual of the suspect?"

"Affirmative. We've got one plain clothes detective inside with eyes on the perp, but no contact."

"Good work, but keep it low profile. We've got FBI close behind, and this is a federal warrant, so they want to make the collar."

"Copy," the officers voice hoarse, "but I'd love to have ten minutes alone with that baby molester." A soft, indistinct curse. "Nothing I hate more'n a guy who diddles kids. I got two girls of my own that I worry some Internet psycho's going to get his hands on."

"We copy that, Sargeant, but this is gonna be one less bastard to worry about. Keep it cool until we arrive."

"Copy, and out."

Harris hung up the mic and looked at his boss whose lips

were knife-slit tight. "This perv goes to the pen, I'm betting he won't last a year," he muttered.

Warner nodded again. "Yeah, Jack. Even the most ruthless cons hate bastards who prey on kids." He grunted. "Wouldn't bother me a bit if someone sticks a shiv between his ribs." He spun the coupe right onto Collins Avenue and spied two patrol cars in the middle of the next block. He ground to a stop at the curb behind a black-and-white and they stepped out. Glancing back, he saw Pauletti's black Suburban just arriving along with Olvida's Chevy.

Agents Pauletti and Whitehead exited the front of their SUV, and tall, blond Ina Yeager stepped from the rear, toting her big sniper rifle. She hurried across the street and found a large trash bin to accept the bipod of the Barret gun, with a clear line of sight to the bistro's front door. No one really expected the need, but she'd be ready, just in case.

Warner, Harris, and the two Fibbies were greeted by a tall, trim, strawberry-hair officer in street blues, three stripes on his arm. Olvida and Beck were hurrying around back of the pub to join patrol cops there. If there were trouble, better the experienced detectives handled it than street cops.

"Sargeant Evers?" Warner asked the man in blue.

He nodded and shook Warner's hand. "All teed up and ready to rumble, Detective." He nodded at the other two. "Agents." Their hands also shook.

"Special Agent in Charge, Pauletti, and this is Special Agent Whitehead." He looked at the Bistro's entry. "The plain clothes guy still inside?"

Evers nodded. "Just got a text that the subject's hitting on a female patron with no success and looks to be getting ready to leave."

"Okay. Agent Whitehead and I will take him down. Post two officers at the door." He glanced at Warner.

"Harris and I will follow you in and fan out ta cover any break he may make to the side." He delivered a light jab to Whitehead's upper arm. "One look at this ex-linebacker should dissuade him from anything."

They all chuckled as they entered into a dimly lit bar, the air surprisingly filled with the scent of jasmine. Apparently, an atomizer at work. Nothing was too good for South Beach. They'd all previewed a photo of their subject and quickly spotted him, just turning away from a long, mahogany bar.

The two agents, walking shoulder-to-shoulder, fronted him, blocking his way.

"Ricardo Macha?" Pauletti said.

"Who's asking?" He planted palms on their chests to stop their advance. "And stop crowding me."

"FBI," Pauletti said, plucking handcuffs from his belt. "You're under arrest for child pornography and illegal sexual contact with minors."

"Hey, what the fuck—" He turned, but Whitehead pinned his arms and spun him around.

"Hands behind your back," Pauletti commanded as he secured his wrists with the cuffs. Turned forward again, one agent on each arm, Warner faced him.

"I'm Chief Detective, Al Warner, and I've also got questions."

"What the fuck?" Macha repeated, brow wrinkled, eyes angry slits.

"I wanna know why you killed Miss Courtney Baines, of Aventura?" His dark eyes bore into Macha's.

"What the fuck?" for a third time. "Who the hell is Courtney Baines?"

"You'll see, once we got'cha in interrogation." He looked at Pauletti. "I want first crack at him, Lon."

"Of course, Detective. Your serial killer case will take

precedence."

"Serial killer?" Macha squawked as they dragged him, stumbling from the bar. "What serial killer? I don't know nothing—"

"You'll have yer chance ta tell us everything, once we get ya to HQ, buddy." Warner began reciting his Miranda Rights, then said, "These nice FBI agents are gonna drive ya in their roomy SUV, and we'll all get together again, after we're back in Miami." He grunted. "Right now, we're honorin' a Virginia warrant for yer arrest."

Warner and Harris lingered at the curb as the perp and the three Fibbies loaded up, Mach secure in the back seats under restraints with Agent Whitehead next to him, ensuring quiet compliance for the ride.

The two detectives reentered Warners Dodge Charger, and Warner fired up the engine, and adjusted the a/c to high. The car had heated up in the midday sun.

"You really think this thug's got any connection to our serial killer, Boss?"

"Don't really see how, Jack. Actually, it wasn't his DNA at the Baines crime scene."

"Yeah. Don't know how that's gonna shake out."

"Right. Pressin' him on that might make him more willin' ta fess up to Pauletti on the baby fuckin' charges. Gotta try to learn why his DNA did turn up during our swabbin' the play's cast members, though." He chuffed as he pulled away from the curb, heading back for the causeway, and Miami. "We gotta find a way to retest those guys. One of 'em figured a way to give us false readin's."

"I wonder if he knew he was giving up DNA from a wanted fugitive, or it was just chance?"

"Good question. We always say we don't believe in coincidence, but sometimes it does happen. Whatever, we got a good collar out of it, and that's one more evil bastard off the streets." He sighed. "Now we gotta figure out where ta go from here.'

Harris nodded, and they continued across the causeway, both lost in thought.

~ 37 ~

Agent Pauletti awaited Warner in the viewing room after the detective finished a ninety-minute interrogation of Ricardo Macha. He turned as Warner entered and joined him at the one-way mirror. They paused, Warner's hands in his pockets, Pauletti's arms interlocked across his chest, and studied their subject, cuffed and slouched at the interrogation room's table.

"So, what d'ya think, Lon? He our guy?"

"Doesn't track, Detective." He glanced at Warner. "He's a bad guy, but I don't think he's our serial killer."

"Yeah, me either." He stroked his jaw as he continued to stare at Macha. "I gotta believe it's one of the guys from that play. I got Harris trackin' 'em all down for another Q & A session here, and we'll make second stab at gettin' fresh DNA samples."

"You able to get warrants for that this time?"

Warner shrugged. "Asked ADA Santamaria ta give it another go. Still waitin' ta hear." He snorted. "Damned judges are gettin' gun-shy after bein' burned on a couple that weren't legit. Some cops oversold the probable cause."

"And if you can't get warrants?" Pauletti's eyebrows arched.

"Gotta figure another way ta get it. We'll have coffee, soft drinks, donuts, and stuff. Tech's just finished settin' up four new CCTV in the conference room, and we'll keep a close watch on who touches what." He grunted and turned from the viewing glass. "Somehow, they're gonna leave some DNA somewhere ... I hope." He headed for the door with the special agent close behind.

"Meanwhile, I'm gonna release Macha inta yer custody, Lon. We've got nothin' on him here, and all the warrants are federal."

"Fine. I've got two agents coming over from the Miami Field Office to pick him up. We'll extradite him to Virginia, where he did most of his dirty work with young girls and is a POI in a murder. He's been on the run for over two years, so they're going to happy to close those cases." He patted Warner on the shoulder as they moved out.

"We've still got a serial killer to take down, and my team wants to be here to help, any way we can."

They paused as Jack Harris intercepted them as they entered the detectives' bullpen. Warner crossed his arms as the short detective stopped and brandished his android tablet.

"Problems, Jack?" Warner asked.

"Yes and no, Boss." His fingers stroked the screen. "I was able to contact the play's director, D'Amato, plus Warwick, our POI, and the producer, Tony Ryder. Looks like the other POI, Travis Mott, has left town."

"Interesting." Warner stroked his chin. "You got a whereabouts on him?"

"Nothing definitive. D'Amato thinks he's got a remote cabin somewhere in the Smokies or Blue Ridge Mountains, but no idea exactly where." He flipped through a few screens then looked up.

"D'Amato and Ryder mentioned another cast member, Josh Scott, who retired after this season and moved to Wyoming, they thought. Another physical match for our perp, and a quiet loner. Both said he was the one member of their crew no one really got to know, so he could be another possibility."

"Text me what you know about him," Pauletti said, "and I'll have our guys run down his history." He looked at Warner. "No way, I guess, to get his DNA unless we track him down."

"D'Amato said he played their innkeeper," Harris said, "and Ryder has all the gear from the show, so maybe we can get something off his costume."

"Worth a try." Warner started for his office. "Been handled by more'n that guy, though, so may not have a clean sample." He rubbed the back of his neck, "But if he's our guy, now in Wyoming, how was he here ta kill Ms. Baines? It don't track."

"True," Agent Pauletti followed him. "But if we have DNA from the others and we get a new reading, it'll probably be Scott's, and that should clear this up. I'll get agents down there to take possession of the costumes."

"Okay. Sound like we got some things workin'. Let's hope we can tie this down and put this bastard away. I hate these shits worse'n anything." Warner entered his office and found his desk piled with new paperwork. He sighed and shrugged. The questionable perks of being chief of detectives.

Agent Pauletti peeled off and headed for his temporary digs in the conference room where he found Agents, Yeager, Solto and Swift, all busy on their phones, working what little they had on their killer. They were getting close, and no proverbial stone would be left unturned.

~ 38 ~

He leaned back, elbows atop the epoxied oak bar-top, and surveyed the room. A sip of his Maker's Mark, neat, and he sighed.

There she was. The black-haired bitch who needed to be punished, but he reluctantly knew he must pass this time. Too dangerous right now with the cops looking over him and the rest of the crew. They'd asked them all to return for some more questioning, and he was sure they were going to make a second try for DNA. He needed to convince the group that, without warrants, they should refuse this time, on the grounds that they didn't want that information available to the public. The cops would assure them it was secure, but they could still refuse out of principle.

Hopefully, with Travis Mott gone, maybe the cops will focus on him as a fugitive. Perfect timing to shift their investigation, and possibly take the heat off me.

He took another sip of his bourbon, eyes riveted on the fortyish, black haired-woman, clearly enjoying herself with two other ladies. He forced his eyes away as hers caught his, and swiveled back to the bar. He spied her in the mirror, still watching him, a small smile twitching at her lips, before giving an elegant shrug and returning her attention to her girlfriends. Clearly, three cougars on the prowl, seeking prey. Predatory bitches, seeming sweet and loving, but really out for domination and abuse.

He knew who she was and what she wanted, and he struggled to control an urge to punish her for her abuses. A small shudder racked him, and he shook his head. Then a soft sigh. Maybe later, if he can deter the police and send them chasing wild geese. The waiters seemed to know her, so she's a regular there, and would be back. No question her stare was filled with interest.

He chuckled under his breath. Somehow, these predatory bitches sensed he was fair game, and he had mastered being exactly that ... right up until they learned differently. And, by then it was too late.

He finished his drink, his second, and dropped a twenty on the bar before sliding off the stool and striding from the hotel's bar. He'd retire to his room and psych himself up for tomorrow's meeting with that super cop, Al Warner. The pack from the FBI will probably be there too. All hands on deck, so he needed to be his very best. Something he trained for all his adult life, ever since he began this quest for retribution.

He could pull it off tomorrow, but if things went awry, his escape plan was teed up and ready to go. He was confident he didn't need to use that, but it was ready, just in case.

~ 39 ~

Warner zipped his pants and turned to the sink to wash his hands when Jack Harris pushed open the door of the squad's men's room.

"They're on their way up, Boss."

"All of them, Jack?"

"D'Amato, Warwick, and Ryder. Had the woman, Bono, come too. Even though we're obviously seeking a guy, maybe she knows something that might help."

"Good thinkin'. Ya got the conference room set up?"

"Yep. The Fibbies have moved out, and we got baskets of donuts and bagels, plus coffee, hot water for tea, and bottles of water all teed up." He ran a hand through his short, sandy hair. "With a bit of luck, we should have what we need to get their DNA."

"Yeah, some luck would be nice, but don't count on it. We may hafta find some other way." He joined Harris as they left the bathroom. "Any word on Mott?"

"The BAU is still digging into his background, but prelim results are pretty vanilla. No criminal record." He fiddled with his Android, searching for a file. "Yeah. Middle-class family and–oh, interesting. Here's a photo of his mom."

Warner accepted the tablet and his eyebrows arched as he viewed the picture. "Attractive, with short, black hair, just like all our vics." He handed it back to Harris. "I presume, based on that, the BAU is diggin' deeper?"

"I'll double-check with Agent Pauletti, Boss."

"Okay. Do that now while I meet with our guest and get started. Agents Yeager and Whitehead are joinin' me in the Q & A. Send Olvida in too."

"On it, Boss." He headed for Agent Pauletti, gathered with a covey of other BAU agents standing around an empty desk in the squad room as Warner continued toward the Conference room. The four cast members were already ensconced inside.

As he approached, he spotted Detective Olvida coming his way. Warner paused, awaiting his arrival, then they entered the room together. The woman and Tony Ryder were settled in chairs, while Nick D'Amato and Clive Warwick fidgeted and paced behind them. Agents Yeager and Whitehead were perched on chairs at the end of the table, donuts and cups of coffee in hand. Hopefully their guests would take the hint.

"Thanks fer comin' back in, folks. I'll try not ta keep ya too long." His gaze swept over the four. "We just need some more input on this case, and you guys are the best link we got so far." He and Olvida settled on chairs and he waved the other two men to sit.

"As you probably know, yer associate, Travis Mott, has left town, and that makes him our number one Person of Interest in these murders." He scanned their faces. "Anything you might know about him that could help?" He gestured at papers on the table. "That's a list of the murders we know of, with dates and times, in case it lights up any memory ya might have about him then."

Tony Ryder picked up the sheets and Warwick and D'Amato hunched close to study them over his shoulder.

"Meanwhile, the FBI's diggin' inta the background and social media history of yer retired member, Josh Scott." He plucked a chocolate donut, took a bite, and shoved the box in front of the seated trio. Only the woman, Bono, accepted the offer, selecting a glazed treat.

"I don't know what more we can tell you, Detective," D'Amato said. "Josh was a loner and rarely joined us in any after-show parties. None of us knew much about him, other than he was a very good actor and was an important member of our cast." He glanced at the other two men, who nodded. "Frankly, looking at this list, I can't say anything for sure about Travis's action then, or anyone else's for that matter." He shrugged as the others murmured agreement. "Unbelievable." He shook his head. "Nineteen women, killed while our play was in each own."

"Yeah. And what about Mott?" Warner's eyebrows arched.

All three shook their heads. Then Clive Warwick said, "He *did* seem like a ladies' man, though, and I know he often visited local bars after the evening shows." He shrugged. "If he's your guy, that coulda been where he'd meet these women."

"Yes," Clara Bono said. "Travis was very charming and loved a good time. Do you think ...?"

"Well," Warner rose and licked chocolate from his fingers. "As I said, his leavin' town makes him our number one guy. The FBI's got a three-state BOLO lookin' for him now." He leaned over the table. "Hold tight fer a minute while I check somethin' with my guys." He nodded toward his people, then waved at the table. "Help yerselves to drinks and snacks. I'll be right back." He turned and headed out the door, aimed for Pauletti and his team, hovered over a desk with a video monitor. Unlike the usual interrogation room, there were no one-way mirrors to view the action, so they were relying on the CCTV cameras.

He circled the desk and viewed the screen, split into four images. He lay a hand on Agent Pauletti's shoulder. "Anything, Lon?"

"Unfortunately, no, Detective." He caught Warner's eyes from the corner of his. "None of the men seem in any way agitated."

"Yeah, well, they're all actors, even the director and producer, so that's no surprise." He studied the images from the room. "And only the woman took the bait of the snacks, so that ain't gonna do us any good ta get DNA." He turned to Pauletti. "Yer guys turn up anything new on any of the guys, includin' Mott and this other guy, Scott?"

"Still digging, but so far, nothing definitive on any of them. Mott, Warwick, even Ryder have histories that *could* fit the mold, but it's all circumstantial at best. Still waiting on the skinny for Scott." He scanned a newly arriving text on his phone. "Looks like the field agents from Miami have picked up Scotts costume from storage and they're sending it up for DNA analysis. Maybe we'll find something there."

"Okay." Warner retrieved his phone from a pocket and hit auto dial for CSU.

"Yes, Detective?" The Hawk's voice was tinged with tolerant humor.

"Bring yer DNA collectin' gear up to the conference room, Moe. We'll see if we can get new samples. Tell 'em the last batch was cross-contaminated or somethin'." He paused. "I'm gonna act like it's a surprise ta me so they won't think it's why we brought 'em back."

"Right. Be there in about 5 or so." He disconnected.

Warner pocketed his phone. "We'll see if we can do this. If not, we'll have ta come up with somethin' else. At this point, DNA is all we got to pinpoint our perp." He shrugged. "If it's not one of these guys, it's gotta be either Mott or Scott." He started for the conference room.

"Good luck," Pauletti called after him. "We'll stay on the monitor to see if someone's actions tell us anything."

Warner nodded and gave a small wave as he strode back

toward the room and it's three POIs. Entering, he plopped on a chair. "Sorry for the small delay, guys. Hadda check somethin' out. Got a few more questions before ya go." He nodded toward the door. "Anyone need a bathroom break?"

All shook their heads.

"So, ya guys looked at the crime list? Nothin' jumps out at ya?"

"No." Warwick rose. "We told you, most of it is too far in the past to remember anything specific." He picked up his cell phone which had been on the table. "If you've got nothing else ...?" Eyebrows arched.

"Okay." Warner also stood. "I'd appreciate it if no one leaves town right now—" He turned as the door popped open and the Hawk entered, wheeling a small metal tray.

"Sorry for interrupting, Detective, but I just learned you had all these people here, and I'd like to ask them for a new round of DNA samples." His dark eyes swept the group. "The last batch somehow got mislabeled, and I don't know who's was who's." His shrug was followed by a grunt. "Very unprofessional of me and my staff." He gathered up three small vials encasing sterile swabs. "So, if you don't mind—"

"Do you have warrants this time?" Clive Warwick asked.

"No-o-o." The Hawk shrugged. "Didn't seem necessary. Last time you all—"

"Yeah, yeah." D'Amato also rose. "But we've all decided not to submit if you asked again."

"We're private people," Clara Bono said. "We're not eager to have our DNA floating around. Besides, why would you even want mine? This killer *is* a man, isn't he?"

"Yes, of course." The Hawk stood, holding the vials. "But I can assure you, there's no public access to this—"

"So you say," Ryder interrupted, "but we still all refuse, on principal. If you want our DNA, you'll need to get a warrant. It's just a fishing expedition, with no real basis."

“But we *do* have that basis,” Warner interjected. “Your play was in town for every one of these murders. That’s more than a coincidence.” He withheld mentioning the Courtney Baines killing, which just happened while the five members of the cast were in Miami.”

“So, get warrants, if you can,” D’Amato said. “Meanwhile, unless you’ve come up with something probative, leave us alone. You’ve already ruined my vacation, and according to what you’ve told us, I don’t even fit the physical profile.”

“Yes,” Ryder added. “It’s been a long, grueling season, and we’d all like a peaceful break. I wouldn’t be surprised if my friends here feel it’s time to move on.” Met with grumbling assent. “South Florida no longer seems welcoming to us, I’m afraid.”

“Yeah, well, we’ve got a serial killer to catch, so we’re just doin’ our jobs too.” Warner stood at the room’s doorway. “I would appreciate you stayin’ in town for at least the next five or six days, though. If ya gotta go, at least leave an address where we can find ya if we have more questions. Or get that DNA warrant.”

“Yeah, okay.” Ryder stepped past Warner and into the doorway. “We got nothing to hide. The DNA just seems like a step too far.” His eyes scanned the others still in the room. “Clara, you want to ride back with me? Clive and Nick may want to go on Lincoln Road for lunch.”

“Yes, thanks Tony. I just wanna go veg on the beach.”

“Okay, let’s go.” He looked at Warner. “Call us, Detective, if you have anything positive to tell us. I don’t think any of us will still be here in four or five days.”

“We’ll be in touch if we need anything else. Enjoy yer stay.” He turned to the Hawk as the door closed behind them.

“Now what, Moe?”

"No one ate or drank anything except the woman, so no joy there."

"Okay." Warner looked at the two BAU agents. "You guys get anything from any of this?"

Agent Yeager looked at Whitehead, and both shrugged. "Nothing we can pin down, Detective. No one seemed excessively nervous, even after you asked for DNA." She glanced at Whitehead. "You pick up any tell, Ansel?"

The man, Pauletti's top profiler, shook his head. "If one of them is our Unsub, he's a very cool customer. The woman seemed the most nervous, and she's not even in the mix."

"Shit." Warner turned to his CSU whiz. "So, Moe, if no one ate anythin, d'ya got any other tricks up those magic sleeves of yours?"

The Hawk's eyes swept the room. "I'm gonna swab the chairs' armrests, and I've got a sterile mini-vac for the seats." He produced two numbered markers from under the cart and lay one in front of Warwick's and Ryder's chairs. "I sterilized everything before they arrived, so whatever we find will be pristine." He withdrew his tiny, battery-powered vacuum and two sterile canisters. "Not gonna bother with D'Amato because he doesn't fit the physical description." He approached the first chair. "Good chance to come up with some skin cells, perspiration, or hairs for each, and this time I'm gonna be damned sure to keep them properly labeled." He donned latex gloves, using a new set for each chair, and went to work.

"How soon, buddy?" Warner watched him operate.

"Once I get everything together, should be two or three days to run accurate tests. I've got two of my best staff teed up and ready to go, once I get all this back to the lab."

"Yeah, well, as fast as ya can, huh. These guys are ready ta boogie, and I got no basis yet ta hold 'em here. Once they're in the wind, we may never find 'em again, and I wanna be the guy to take this sonofabitch down." He gave a soft growl. "Four vics in my neck of the woods don't sit well with me."

"Believe me, I know that about you, Detective. We'll work fast as we can without jeopardizing the results. You'll be the first to hear." He turned to the chair used by Warwick and began vacuuming the seat. Swabs sat on the desk, ready for the chair arms.

Nothing would be left to chance this time.

Warner watched him work for a few minutes, then left for his office. He still had a pile of paperwork to sort through and an after-action report to write.

His very favorite part of being Chief Homicide Detective.

~ 40 ~

Warner hunched over his weathered oak desk, forearms resting on its scarred surface, as he clicked on his desktop's mouse and scrolled though the report on Travis Mott. Agent Pauletti had sent over files on Mott, Warwick, and even Tony Ryder, the play's producer. All three men met the physical description of their perp. Their psych profiles were another matter. With Mott now in the wind, he seemed the most obvious one to review first. But Pauletti's cover e-mail indicated all three had thought-provoking histories.

Hmm. Interestin'. Travis Mott had changed his name. Born Thomas Krona. Father unknown. Taken by CPS from his mother, who was adjudicated as unfit: an alcoholic hooker. Three different foster families until he finally stuck at the age of nine. Seemed like good people who put him through school with a drama degree at a Cincinnati city college. Changed his name to Travis Mott while in college.

"Looks like life wasn't all peaches and cream for Mr. Mott," Warner muttered. Lots of angry rants about his family while away at school. Something was going on between him and his foster mom, with lots of nasty Facebook posts from his foster dad which he reacted to in kind.

Strange they had him for twelve years but never moved to adopt him. Everything ended in angry tirades on both sides, and they split, with virtually no further connection after he graduated. That's when he changed his name. Was there an innuendo of a sexual relationship with the woman?

Some of the husband's posts to Mott? The BAU thought our perp may have been molested by an older woman as a child. Mott's history seemed to tell that story.

Warner scrolled though the man's file. Never married. The Feds discovered three relationships for the guy, all with older women, but nothing for the last ten years, after he joined the play's cast. About the same time as the first murder of a 40's, black-haired woman tied to their serial killer in Richmond, Virginia.

All things, combined with his disappearing, made Mott look more and more like their perp. Right height, right build, and a goodlooking actor who probably knew how to lay down a convincing line to a gullible babe.

Almost too good ta be true. Always meticulous, Warner shrugged and brought up Clive Warwick's file. They already knew he had big time issues with his father and mother before they died in a fiery car crash, the cause of which was never fully determined. According to the accident report, their brakes failed during an I-95 traffic stoppage, and the car plowed into and under the rear of a stopped semi, trapping the couple inside as the car burst into flames. A gristly way to die.

He was married, then bitterly divorced after his wife caught him with high-end escorts—twice. No kids, and no record of any violent activity, but Warner knew many serial killers like their current perp were sometimes slow to evolve. Physically, he matched what they knew about their killer, but all three of these men qualified in that area.

Warner scrolled through Warwick's social media history, as complied in detail by the Feds, but nothing stood out. He reviewed the BAU's assessment, and in the end, it was noncommittal: nothing damning there, but nor was it dismissive. Less social media content than Mott, but did they seem edged with ... what? Anger? No. More like bitterness toward the women in his life, maybe with a feeling of being used. Possible motives for delayed revenge? Maybe.

Slumped back in his chair, Warner massaged his eyes and emitted a soft groan. This was going nowhere without a DNA match to clearly point them to a subject. He sighed, straightened, scrolled back, and reread Warwick's file, hoping to find something he'd missed. The guy was his original main POI, but without anything substantive, he was just a "possible."

"Shit." Muttered as he minimized the file and brought up Tony Ryder's, the thinnest if the three. He paged down past his physical info, which like Mott and Warwick, fit their perp. Forty-five, and as Warner recalled, smooth and the calmest of the bunch, and most cooperative. He'd provided Mott's costume for a DNA search, and those results, along with whatever the Hawk had garnered from their last meeting, were still pending. Gold had informed him yesterday that he had minute samples to work with, and it was going to take some time to get it right. Warner snorted. *If it takes too long, we might be fillin' another body bag.*

He sighed and returned his gaze to the screen. *Hmm.* Strange. He returned to Mott's profile to verify what he'd skipped over. *Yeah.* Their wayward actor's foster parents had also died prematurely. House fire at night, blamed on a faulty gas heater in their bedroom.

Interesting coincidence that all three guys' parents died of unnatural causes. According to his file, Ryder's parents perished as the result of a murder/suicide, the mother leaving a note accusing her husband of blatant adultery. A year later Ryder left the off-Broadway show he was producing and joined the traveling play. His Facebook posts at the time said he couldn't bear to stay in one place after his dear parents died so tragically.

Warner knuckled his eyes and sat back, gazing at the

screen. There had to be something they were missing.

Of course! He snatched up his phone and hit an auto dial number.

"Pauletti," was the voice answering. "What can I do for you, Detective?"

"I'm goin' over the three guys' profiles ya sent me, Lon, and noticed all of their parents died violently. Each unsolved and all at a time that mighta caused an acceleration of behavior. Don't see anything like social media from any of the parents. No histories or in-depth backgrounds. You do any?"

"Smart catch, Al. Actually, we were running those backgrounds as well, but I wanted to get you what we had on our POI's first. I think those parents' backgrounds may have just been finished. I'll send over whatever we've got now, and expedite what's not yet completed." He paused. "There's a good chance that parental interaction may have had a causal effect on setting our killer off. I'll have my team go over it as well."

"Great," Warner said. "If the parents are the trigger, good chance our perp may have killed them, too. How soon will I have 'em?"

"Just pulling up what I've got now. They'll be in your e-mail in the next minute or two."

"Thanks. I'll get right on 'em, and let me know if your guys come up with anything, as well."

"Copy that, Detective. Here they come. Call me if anything strikes you."

"You'll be my first call. I'm gonna open the files now. Talk later." Warner disconnected and opened his e-mail register, finding the new message right at the top. He opened it, downloaded three files, and began scanning, jotting a few notes on a lined pad as he went. Very interesting reading.

Deeply engrossed, he started at sudden trill of his

phone. Caller ID showed FORENSICS. He plucked it up and tapped ANSWER.

"Moe. Good news, I hope."

"Mixed, Detective. I've finished running all three DNAs. Unfortunately, due to the very small and partially corrupted samples, I wasn't able to achieve better than a 60% match."

"Better'n nothin', buddy. So, ya got one with a partial match? Who is it?"

"I don't want you running off with this half-cocked, Al. It's not a sure enough link, and any good defense attorney will tear it apart in court. You'll need more than—"

"Yeah, yeah, I know. Once I got someone ta focus on, I'll get the rest. Who is it?"

The Hawk relayed a name, and Warner jotted it down in large caps. *Well, what d'ya know.* His fingers found the X-shaped scar under his curly hair above his right ear. Always got itchy when he was close to solving a case. Turning back to his computer, he printed out the e-mail pages covering his probable perp's parents and began reading, looking for something to put the proverbial nail into his coffin. He hummed softly to himself when things began coming together as he read.

"Damn," he muttered. "We had this whole thing upside down. What a surprise." He rose and strode to his door.

"Harris, Olvida," yelled. "In here."

"Coming, Boss." In chorus.

Returning to his desk, he called Special Agent in Charge Pauletti again. "Lon, we got a partial DNA hit on our guy, and I'm formulatin' a plan on how ta tie him down. C'mon over, ASAP, and I'll run it by ya. Yer the psych crew, so I'll need yer input ta see if ya think it'll work."

"We're at the Miami field office, Detective. Should be there within fifteen minutes. Who is it?"

"Tell ya when ya get here. Bring yer whole crew. The more heads the better on this. We got him, Lon, and I don't want him slippin' away."

"Copy that. See you soon."

Disconnected, Warner turned to his door as Detectives Harris and Olvida pushed in.

"What's up, Boss?" Harris asked.

"The Hawk's got a partial DNA match for our perp."

"One of our three guys?" Olvida's eyebrows arched

"Yep, but we're gonna need more ta tie him down. I need ya both ta bring 'em in ASAP, before he slips away."

"All of them, Boss?" Harris scratched his cheek. "Who's our guy?"

Warner told them, then said, "We need all three, though, ta make this work."

"How you plan to do that, Boss?" Olvida asked.

"By stealin' a scene from their play." He chuckled. "Gonna run it by the BAU crowd who'll be here soon, and see what they think, but I'm bettin' this'll work." He waved a dismissive hand. "So, scoot. I need all three guys fer this ta work, I think. Go get 'em."

The two men hurried off, and Warner settled back at his desk and began again reading the parents' file of the man he was now sure was their serial killer. He needed to know everything, said and intimated, to make this succeed.

~ 41 ~

He beeped off his car's alarm, slid onto the seat, and reclined the back. Eyes closed, he massaged his temples and breathed a soft groan. He removed the prosthetic eyebrows and black, shoulder-length wig, and peeled off the small bump atop his nose. The black-haired witch had physically drained him. Twice, and sorely tested his resolve in the process.

He'd lost a struggle with his better judgement and returned to the beachside bar. Mixed emotions erupted when he spied the woman he'd seen there before, surely another heartless bitch sorely in need of punishment. On a stool at the bar, she sipped her probable martini, alone, eyes surveying the room. He spied a glint there when she noticed his arrival, and he moved in, perching on the next seat.

It didn't take long before she broke the silence with a soft, witty comment. They fenced and preened, all the time he knowing she was seeking an opening to eventually abuse him. In less than an hour, peppered by tête-à-tête and some sensual slow dances, they left for a nearby hotel in Miami Beach. He followed her Acura in his car, knowing he'd need his own wheels once they were done ... no matter what those results were.

Ivana Carlyle was everything he'd expected. Gorgeous, passionate, and domineering. The sex, and what incredible sex it was, centered around her in the lead: teasing, tempting, arousing, and in total control. He played the submissive lover to her dominant control, because that's who she was—an evil, heartless woman.

After his second orgasm, she perched across his groin, trading kisses. His hands stroked her lovely curves as they ventured to her throat, thumbs caressing it. So easy then to squeeze the life from her, a reward for proving who she really was.

Teeth gritted, a struggle within ensued as he fought down the clear need to punish this woman for her heartlessness. He knew bringing her to justice would expose him to that dogged cop, Al Warner, and that realization withered any passion still in him. Instead, he pulled her down for soft kisses and warm cuddling, then made apologies for having to leave, citing an early morning business meeting, and then an urgent appointment out of town that afternoon.

Ivana was petulant in her disappointment, hoping he'd stay the night, but he knew if he lingered longer, he might be unable to control his need to extract retribution. He promised to call her when he returned, something he intended to do, once the heat died down. With Travis Mott now the cop's main person of interest, he may be in the clear for now. If-and-when they discovered their error, he planned to be long gone to a place where no one would find him.

They'd kissed and hugged, her bare skin pressed against him, fingers playing at his crotch as they lingered at the door. The bitch was a succubus, arousing his murderous ardor, but he fought it down and left with a slip of paper thrust into his pocket with her address and phone number scrawled on it.

He straightened in his car's seat and fired up the engine, thoughts of passion and punishment roughly thrust aside. Time to get to his room, catch a few winks, and then pack and leave. Get going while the going was still good.

A glance in his mirror as he drove off, his tongue swiped

dry lips. He'd definitely return some day when it's safe. One more glorious romp with that sexy bitch before teaching her the error of her ways. He just had to await the right time.

He'd slept later than he intended, so drained by the woman the previous evening. Back now from breakfast at the hotel's restaurant, he'd begun to pack. Just a small, wheeled suitcase and a duffle full of some of the play's costumes and makeup, his disguise portfolio.

A chill sent goose bumps down his back at an unexpected knock at his door.

"Who's there?" He closed the case and slid both bags under the bed.

"Detective Harris. You got a minute?"

"Just a sec, while I get dressed." He scooted to his window, which gave a view of the hotel's front entrance. He spotted an unmarked car at the front door with the other two men from the play hovering nearby.

What the hell? Bringing us all in a third time for more questions? I thought with Mott in the wind ... He sighed. With all of them going, no arrests seemed likely. Once more into the breech before he could hit the road. He strode to the door and opened it.

"What can I do for you detective? I thought you had your man. Travis Mott, right?"

"Yeah, he's our top person of interest, but my boss wants a few more minutes with all three of your, just to tie up a few loose threads." Harris glanced at his watch. "Should have you back before lunch."

"Okay, I guess." He turned back to the room. "Give me a minute to get organized and I'll meet you at your headquarters."

"You don't mind, I'll wait. The boss wants me to chauffer the three of you in my car." He chuckled. "Never pays to argue with Al Warner."

"Okay, okay. Let me get my things and I'll meet you in the lobby."

"I'll wait here for you, and we can go down together."

The man shrugged, closed the door, and stepped to the dresser to pick up his wallet and keys. *Shit. He doesn't want me out of his sight. Aren't they centered on Mott? Oh, well. Play it cool. They're fishing, and I'm not gonna bite.*

Five minutes later, the three men were in Harris's car, headed for Miami-Dade HQ.

~ 42 ~

The four men climbed the steps and entered the Miami-Dade's detective squad room, each wondering why they were here ... again. With Travis Mott their main Person of Interest, what more could they add? Jack Harris herded them into the detectives' bullpen.

"We're gonna be using the same conference room," Harris said, "so go ahead in and make yourselves comfortable. I'll tell the Boss you're here." He gestured toward the room. "May be a couple of BAU agents there already, but nothing to get up tight about." He watched them pick their way across the room, then turned and strode toward Warner's office, his lips slit in a grim smile. *If I know the boss, someone's gonna be very uptight pretty soon.* A moment later, he rapped on Warner's door.

The Chief of Detectives glanced up from where he was jotting on a note pad and nodded.

"They here, Jack?"

"Yeah, Boss." He entered and settled on a chair. "Headed to the conference room. Agents Pauletti, Whitehead, and Yeager are there, teed up and waiting for them."

"Okay, let 'em stew for a few." He scanned his computer's monitor and scrawled something on the white, lined pad. "Just gettin' my ducks in a row."

Harris nodded. "From what I've seen, we don't have enough ducks to pin this on anyone yet, do we?"

"Nothin' yet that the DA would like, 'cause it's all circumstantial, but I *know* who our culprit is now." He leaned back and ran a hand through his curly, dark hair. "I just gotta make that plain to him, and maybe he'll spill—intentionally or not."

"So, how are you going to do that." Harris leaned forward. "Not likely he's gonna confess."

"Ya wouldn't think so, but I've discussed this with Eva. She's as good a shrink as the Fibbies got, and we've gone over how ta approach it. With some luck ..." He trailed off. "Anyhow, I got my notes and my story, and we'll see how it goes. I plan on nailin' the bastard today." He rose and gathered up the pad and his phone.

Harris also stood. "You said the BAU got it worked out why he was killing the women and sticking a knife in their hearts?"

"Yeah, we all did, in a sense. He's punishin' these women for havin' an 'evil heart,' but not why we first thought." Warner headed out his door. "C'mon, let's get to it. I got a killer ta nail."

Harris trailed his boss as they strode across the bullpen and pushed into the squad room. Their three subjects sat together on the other side of the long, oval table, and the FBI agents perched to Warner's left, at the far end. Agents Pauletti and Whitehead had laptops open and poised ready to upload files to the 65" plasma TV, mounted on the other wall.

"Hi, gents," Warner settled onto a chair, Harris perched to one side. "Thanks for comin' in on such short notice."

"This is getting kinda overdone, Detective," Clive Warwick said as his eyes swept the room. "We thought you had your killer in Travis Mott, although the idea any of us may have been involved in these gristly crimes is stunning."

"Yeah, well, I can see why that might bother ya, but the fact is, your play was showin' *every single time* one of these women was killed. We *know* it was someone from yer crew."

He scanned his notes. “Same physical description each time. Height and build that’d fit Mott alright, but also you, Mr. Warwick, and even Mr. Ryder.” He leaned back. “Our perp is also an expert at disguise, usin’ different wigs and facial prosthetics ta change his appearance. Good enough ta confound any facial rec programs with the limited views we had of him through CCTV cams. Somethin’ an actor would be good at.”

“C’mon,” Nick D’Amato pitched in, “I know I’m not a suspect because I *don’t* fit that physical description, so I don’t even know why I’m here. But what kind of motive can anyone have for doing these horrible things?” He glanced at his two friends. “I’ve known these guys forever. Mott, too. I can’t believe—”

“I get it, sir,” Warner said, “and yer here as a curtesy for when we tie it all together.” His eyes swept over the three, “but the fact is, one of yer people, I’m sure much ta yer surprise, is a murderer ... and it *ain’t* Travis Mott!”

“What?” Blurted in chorus from the three men, all of whom stiffened in their chairs.

“But we thought—” D’Amato was cut off by Warner.

“I know what ya thought. I *know* what the killer *wanted* us ta think, but with the help of my very capable friends from the FBI,” nodding at the three agents, “who dug far deeper inta yer backgrounds than I bet ya ever imagined, we figured it out.” He paused, dark eyes probing Warwick and Ryder.

“Made sense it’d be an actor. Someone familiar with disguises and makeup. Someone who could pitch a smooth line to a gullible woman. Someone whose mother had short, black hair.” He grunted and glanced again at his notes. “The latter was of no value, unfortunately. It woulda made figurin’ this out a lot easier, but both you guys’ mothers fit that description.” He sighed, then leaned forward, forearms resting on the table.

"And both yer parents were far from perfect, weren't they?" He riveted Warwick with his gaze. "Yer dad was a nasty drunk, a guy who beat both you and yer mom. Ya got outta there while still in yer late teens after ya laid him out. The arrest report said ya had a roll of nickels in yer hand when ya smacked him. Shows ya thought ahead, so it was premeditated assault and battery." He nodded again at Pauletti, and a copy of his arrest warrant and eventual adjudication flashed onto the big screen. "Lucky ya had a sympathetic judge who just gave ya three years of probation." Warner gave a tight grin. "Managed ta keep yer nose clean after that and got inta actin'. And here we are."

"You're crazy," Warwick growled. "I didn't kill any women, and you've got no evidence I did, do you?" He rose. "I want an attorney."

"Okay, but why don't ya wait until I'm finished. I ain't talked yet about yer buddy, there," nodding at Ryder, who looked away and squelched a small, growing smile.

"And so we got Mr. Ryder. A very helpful guy. Got us Motts costumes for a DNA check." Warner fastened his gaze on the man as he eased back in his chair. "A guy whose mom fits our vic profiles too, and with a very unhappy childhood."

"So what? That doesn't make me a killer."

"No, not per se." Warner shuffled a few papers, then looked at Pauletti, and again nodded.

The agent typed on his lap top, and Warwick's documents disappeared from the plasma screen, followed by a display of a series of old, MySpace posts, beginning in 2005. Warner activated a laser pen and highlighted the first one. "This was yer first Internet rant about yer dear mom. As we can see, ya were pretty bitter that, after all these years, she still made excuses fer what happened."

"Yeah." Ryder squirmed in his chair. "But I don't know anyone who doesn't have something to bitch about with their parents." His right thumb was busy with the other fingers on that hand.

"Maybe," Warner grunted and swiped fingers across his lips, "but you had more'n yer fair share, didn't ya?"

The red dot from his laser skipped over several of the posts and Pauletti slowly scrolled through the over a dozen they'd copied.

"Lots of anger at both parents. After the psych experts at the FBI's BAU analyzed these, and some earlier e-mails to yer mom and dad, it's clear why ya were so mad." His dark eyes held Ryders, which were beginning to water.

"Daddy denigrated you for going ta acting classes and then seekin' a degree in drama. We got stuff where, as a preteen and later, he called ya 'pretty boy' and 'girly boy'. You were his sweet little girl, weren't ya?"

Ryder groaned, hands pressed against his temples, eyes shut, but he said nothing.

"Yer daddy loved his little girl, didn't he?" This was the plot Eva and he had designed.

Ryder again said nothing, eyes clamped shut, panting softly.

"He loved ya so much, he took ya to his bed."

"No-o-o," hissed from Ryder.

"He made you perform oral sex, and even fucked ya, didn't he? Fucked ya in the ass, while momma did nothin'. Nothin' ta protect her only boy."

"No-o-o! No-o-o!" Eyes now overflowing.

Warner went on, as Warwick and D'Amato edged their chairs away, putting distance between them and the anguished man.

"Yer pop was evil, committin' sodomy with his son, but it was yer mom ya blamed for not protectin' ya." Warner paused. "It was her who had the evil heart in yer eyes, wasn't it?"

Ryder raised his eyes to Warner's, glittering with anger.

"She could have stopped him, the evil bitch!" he hissed, his face screwed into an angry scowl, his eyes now dry. "She was just happy he turned his attention away from her. That's why she killed him, then shot herself." He slumped in his chair.

"Yeah, maybe. But that was years later, after his continued wild affairs with other women ... and men. The Feds found it all." Warner leaned in. "She coulda ended it earlier ta protect you, but never did. Ya never forgave her fer that, did ya?"

"Forgive her?" Ryder growled. "Forgive her? She didn't deserve forgiveness. The bitch stood by and watched him abuse me. She was evil!"

"Evil, with an evil heart. Right?"

Ryder looked away and said nothing.

"All women like her: same age, same body, same hair— they deserve to die. Have their evil hearts stilled forever."

Ryder stared down but said nothing.

"Ya sulked, filled with anger. Filled with hate." Warner picked up a paper. "Then ten years ago, ya found Rose Jensen. A knockoff of yer mom: early 40's, short black hair, nubile bod." His black orbs riveted Ryder, whose eyes were downturned. "It started just as an affair fer ten-days, while ya directed the plays first venue. But then something changed, and—"

"Yeah," a quiet growl, lips a knife slit. "She thought she was gonna be my dom."

Warner nodded. "What ya didn't know, I'm guessin', was she made MySpace posts about her hot new toy, in town, directin' a mystery play." He eased back and folded his arms.

"We were just lovers—"

"Until she brought out her toys: handcuffs, masks, whips." Warner shook his head. "Local police reports had it as an affair that got outta hand. A one-time thing. But it was the trigger that set ya off, wasn't it?"

"No, no. I just ended it—"

'Yeah, by killin' her fer bein' an evil woman, just like yer mom."

Ryder said nothing, eyes down, body quaking.

"The FBI got DNA offa mask and cuffs, still in the local evidence locker. Their techs work miracles. Matched our killer's, but somehow, ya managed to feed us Ricardo Macha's instead of yers, fer which, by-the-way, we thank ya. An unexpected bust." He swiveled his gaze toward the door and the Hawk wheeled in his little cart.

"But now, we're gonna get yer real DNA as the final link to our killer. Nineteen women, finally avenged."

Ryder scrunched back in his chair. "I refuse to submit—"

"No choice this time, bub." Warner rose. "We got a warrant, don't we, Jack?" He glanced at Harris who held up his phone.

"Just got the text confirmation, Boss."

Warner nodded to the Hawk. "And I expect it's also gonna tie up the fact that yer parents *weren't* a murder/suicide, but a double murder by you, right after ya killed Rose Jensen. Her death was the provocation to set everything 'right' in yer mind. They *all* had ta be punished."

Ryder lurched out of his chair, eyes wildly sweeping the room.

Jack Harris materialized behind him, trapping his flailing arms and applying cuffs.

"Tony Ryder, you're under arrest for the murder of Courtney Baines and eighteen other women to be later named. Anything you say may be used against you ..." rattling off the familiar Miranda wording.

Warner helped Harris immobilize the man while the Hawk collected his DNA. Then Harris led him off as Warner turned back to the special agents still in the room.

"Good job, guys, in diggin' up all those past posts. They were the final nails."

"Well, nothing ever really goes away on the Internet," Agent Yeager said. "It just takes some talented individuals to unearth them."

"Somethin' you guys got an abundance of. Talented techs." Warner chuckled and patted Pauletti arm.

"Your wife had some pretty good insights here, too, Detective," Pauletti said as he gathered up is laptop and papers.

"Yeah, she's helped me a lot with cases, and prepped me on this line of questioning. We had no facts about the abuse, but she suspected if we pushed it, he might crack."

"Smart lady," Yeager said. "She was right on the mark in both the Prom Dress Killer and the Sniper cases too."

"Well, one more in the books," Warner said, starting for the door. He gave a wry chuckle. "Three, actually. Our serial killer, Macha, the pedophile, and a ten-year-old double murder, disguised as a murder/suicide." He grunted. "At least this time, I didn't have ta fight the guy fer my life."

"Yeah," Yeager said. "No need for me to have to save your ass for a change."

They all chuckled.

"Yes, a pretty good day." Pauletti clapped him on the back as they strode into the detective's bullpen.

Detective Harris intercepted Warner as he headed toward his office.

"What's up, Jack?"

"We frisked Ryder to be sure he was clean and found this, Boss." He handed something to Warner. "Thought you might want to do something with it."

"Wow." He handed it back to his detective. "Better check it out ta be sure we got no more problems there, then get it back ta me." He rubbed his jaw. "Don't think we should ignore it, no matter what."

"On it, Boss," and he headed for his desk. Shouldn't take very long to track down.

Epilogue

Eva entered their townhome and crossed into the den where she spied her husband, Al Warner, sprawled out on his recliner chair, hands clasped across his belly, eyes closed. but not asleep. He stirred, raised his head, and grinned.

"Hey, babe. Home early, huh?"

"Not as early as you, I see." She crossed the room, settled on his lap, and planted a lingering kiss on his lips. She cocked her head. "Where's Andrea, hon?"

"The munchkin? With Adele, probably bakin' pies, if I know my feisty, old neighbor." He grinned. "Said she'd keep her fer the evenin'."

"So, I suspect this means the case is closed?" She caressed his cheek.

He straightened the chair, she still on his lap, his arms circling her waist, and gave a more passionate kiss. Head tilted back, fingers of one hand in her ruby locks, he grinned. "Hard ta think about a case when I've got this gorgeous redhead perched on my lap, makin' out with me, but yeah. Ran the game we devised, and faced with everything, he cracked. The DNA from his first murder was the clincher." He reached into his shirt pocket and extracted a piece of paper.

"I got a favor ta ask." He handed her the slip.

"What's this?"

"The address and phone number of a Ms. Ivana Carlyle."

Eva's eyebrows arched. "And ...?"

"We took it off Ryder after the collar."

"Is she ...?"

"Alive? Yeah, we checked, but we thought she should know how close she came. A warning ta be careful in the future."

"So, what? You want *me* to call her?"

"I can do it, if yer reluctant, but I thought it might be better comin' from a woman, and who better'n you to deliver the message?"

"Of course, I will. You're probably right, and I don't mind."

"Great. That's one of the reasons I love ya so much." He rose, Eva cradled in his grasp, her arms linked around his neck. "So, once we got Ryder in custody and I finished all the paperwork, I decided to come home early." He strode across the room.

"Where are we headed, lover?" Her lips teased into a soft grin, and she pecked his nose.

"Fer the bedroom, darlin'. I figured, after catchin' the bastard who killed nineteen lovely women, I deserved a treat."

"Did you, now?" A soft, breathy chuckle. "What d'ya have in mind?"

"Ya know damned well what that is, you tease." He pushed through the bedroom doorway. "Really happy yer home early, babe."

"No accident, sweetheart." She sighed as he lay her on the bed and sat beside her. "I called your department to see how things were going, and they gave me the news and told me you took off early."

"Really?" Grinning as he began shedding his duds.

"Yeas, really." She slipped off her short-sleeved blouse and began shimmying out of her skirt. "You've been so distracted by this case that we haven't—"

"Shh." Her words stilled by his lips. "We can talk later. Now I just wanna make love to my most perfect woman." Both nude except for undies, Warner slid atop of her, his lips and fingers erotic venturers. Soon they were lost in the throes of passion and pleasure, all thoughts of the world around them momentarily stilled.

Thirty minutes later, they lay snuggled together, her head in the crook of his neck.

Warner sighed and gave Eva a soft squeeze. "Strange thing about people."

"What? That a man can be so traumatized in his youth, but waits twenty years to begin extracting vengeance, and that on innocent women? The mind's a complex thing, Al."

"Yeah, of course. No one probably knows that better'n you, darlin'." He paused. "But it's how differently people react."

"You're thinking of your youth, aren't you?" She wiggled up and propped her chin on her hand, elbow braced on the bed.

"Yeah, I guess." On his side, he faced her. "It wasn't so different than Ryder's. My pop never raped me, but he was a brutal sonofabitch who dealt out plenty of physical punishment. Both me and mom, but mostly aimed at me."

"And your mom did nothing to stop him, just like Ryder's. Right?"

"Yep. She abided it and never said a word. You know the rest. Once I got big enough, I took away his whip and drove him off. She never said a word. Just tended our minnow and bait shop ... and ignored me. I was on the wrong road—into punks and gangs—until my math teacher and a cop took me under their wings." He sighed, leaned down for a gentle kiss, then continued. "With letters of recommendation from them, I bugged out. Couldn't get far enough away from Antioch, Illinois."

"Yes. You came right to Florida."

"Yeah. Like I said, far away as possible." He grunted. "Applied to the Miami Beach Police Academy. Six years on patrol, then took the Detective's exam."

"And now you're Miami-Dade Chief of Detectives, catching murders and serial killers, and no one does it better, not even the FBI." They sat together on the bed, holding hands. "And, by the way, you're my wonderful, tender husband, and one hell of a great lover." She wrapped him in her arms, their warm bodies moving together, lips strolling on sensual adventures.

Soon they again soared into Nirvana, lost in tender yet intense passion.

As always, he never ceased to marvel that this incredible, classy woman fell in love with him. He was filled with glorious awe as they neared climax.

"Oh, God!" she gasped as she shuddered with her orgasm.

Finished finally, snuggled together under sheets, they slept. Their world was at peace again.

At least for the moment.

~ The End ~

www.ingramcontent.com/pod-product-compliance
Lightning Source LLC
LaVergne TN
LVHW090603110826
845146LV00001B/238

* 9 7 9 8 9 8 7 1 6 0 7 3 2 *